KIDS WITHOUT HOMES

Also by Joan J. Johnson

AMERICA'S WAR ON DRUGS

KIDS WITHOUT HOMES

BY JOAN J. JOHNSON

FRANKLIN WATTS
NEW YORK/LONDON/TORONTO/SYDNEY/1991

Photographs copyright ©: Impact Visuals: pp. 13 (Amy Zuckerman), 45 (T.L. Litt), 60, 161 (both George Cohen), 82 (Les Stone); The Bettmann Archive: pp. 20, 32 bottom; Photo Researchers, Inc.: 32 top (Susan Kuklin), 104 (Blair Seitz), 121 (Arthur Tress); Jim Hubbard/Shooting Back, Educational Media Center: pp. 36 (Jim Hubbard), 99 (Charlene Williams); Gamma-Liaison: 41 (Yvonne Hemsey), 119 bottom (Bruce Hoertel), 153 (George Cohen); David M. Grossman: pp. 65, 169; Rhoda Galyn: p. 73; Emergency Lodge Play School, Salvation Army, Chicago: p. 94; Monkmeyer Press Photo: p. 110 (George Janecek); Woodfin Camp & Associates: pp. 119 top (Wally McNamee), 164 (Jacques Chenet).

Library of Congress Cataloging-in-Publication Data
Johnson, Joan J.
Kids without homes / by Joan J. Johnson.
p. cm.
Includes bibliographical references and index.
Summary: Examines homelessness in today's society as it affects our nation's youth, their education, upbringing, opportunities for employment, enmeshment with crime, and prospects for ameliorating their situation.
ISBN 0-531-11064-8 (lib. bdg.)—ISBN 0-531-15228-6
1. Homeless youth—United States—Juvenile literature.
2. Homelessness—United States—Juvenile literature. 3. Homeless persons—Services for—United States—Juvenile literature.
[1. Homeless persons. 2. Homelessness.] I. Title.
HV4505.J64 1991
362.7'08'6942—dc20 91-12847
CIP
AC

Printed in the United States of America
6 5 4 3 2

CONTENTS

KIDS WITHOUT HOMES

CHAPTER 1
THE CONSEQUENCE OF POVERTY

For six months after Jessica's father died in 1989, she lived with her mother, brother, and baby sister Sheina in a small apartment in the South Bronx, part of New York City. Then the City Health Department condemned it and ordered them to leave. The apartment was infested with city rats—huge, often aggressive, rodents that have little fear of humans. According to the *New York Times,* Jessica's mother stayed up at night to watch over Sheina after she found a rat in the baby's crib. Rats, which carry a variety of diseases, are especially drawn to the smell of milk in babies' bottles and have been known to bite small children. It is said that they are probably responsible for more human deaths than all the wars in history. Jessica and her five-year-old brother Christopher were also frightened by the rats, and on some nights, they stayed awake with their mother because they were afraid to sleep. At school, Jessica and Christopher were tired and listless. Jessica tried to do her schoolwork, but she often nodded off with the pencil in her hand. Her teacher called home, asking if Jessica was getting enough sleep at night. Christopher even imagined he was seeing rats at school. The thoughts frequently made him throw up. He began destroying toys.

When the City Health Department stepped in and closed her family's apartment, Jessica's mother had no place to go. She could not afford a better apartment or a better neighborhood. She was a single mother with three children to care for. She had no choice. She brought her family to a shelter. Jessica, Christopher, and Sheina became kids without a home.[1]

Rosie Slusher's desire to protect her four children from another kind of danger led them to Sister Connie Driscoll's shelter in Chicago, Illinois. They, too, tried to survive in the cheapest apartment they could find, in a public housing development. Unfortunately, public housing, like private tenements in the slums, is often rife with violence and crime. Someone threw bleach in the face of Rosie's eleven-year-old daughter. Her nine-year-old child was thrown down the stairs. According to an article in *U.S. News & World Report,* Mrs. Slusher looked everywhere for a safer place to raise her family, but the apartments she could afford were no better than what she had—rooms with the ceilings caving in, many of them rat- and roach-infested. Mrs. Slusher had no alternative either. She and her family became homeless.[2]

Shelley, Jennifer, and Christine Klatt live in a tent in Orange County, California. Their mother, Ms. Lawson, was evicted from her Ontario, Canada, home in March 1989. The family set up camp at Yorba Linda's Featherly Regional Park because they had no place to live, nor could they afford one. Ms. Lawson had been unemployed since June 1988. She had payments due on their truck, their only means of transportation. She had back bills to pay. She told the Orange County, California *Register* that living in a camp was the only thing she could afford. The girls shower and dress in the campground's public restroom. They eat their meals at a picnic table, except when it rains. On those days, they eat in their tent. They go to nearby St. Joseph's Upland School each day and pretend they are like the other children. They wear the school uniform. They laugh and giggle with their classmates. But when would-be friends want their telephone number or ask their address, they give vague answers because they are ashamed.[3]

When Leandra Cordiva's husband lost his job in an auto parts store, they could no longer stay in their home. She contacted the public housing authority only to learn that the waiting list for publicly assisted apartments was so long that she would have to wait two years before a place to live became available. For a while, the Cordivas and their seven children tried to split up, living with relatives who took them in. But living off relatives and being separated led to such unbearable tension and arguments that the Cordivas finally decided to go to a shelter. At least there they could be together. They went to the Star of Hope shelter in Houston, Texas. At the Star of Hope, one child told a Houston, Texas *Chronicle* reporter, "I've been here so long, I'm not sure how long I've been here."[4]

Julian Summers is sixteen. His mother, sister, and four-month-old nephew have been homeless since Julian was eleven. They are among those living at the Pitts Motor Hotel in Maryland. An older and a younger brother live with their grandmother in Silver Spring, Maryland. "It's pretty bad being homeless," Julian told the *Washington Post.* Each morning, the family must pack their belongings in garbage bags and wait for a bus to pick them up and take them to the Pitts Hotel for breakfast. After that, they have nothing to do but wait for lunch, then dinner, then their return to sleeping quarters. They are among the thousands of homeless families housed at motels and hotels in cities and towns across the nation because permanent welfare housing is filled.[5]

Autumn is two months old. She lives with her eighteen-year-old mother and her mother's boyfriend, Steve, in Covenant House in Fort Lauderdale, Florida, a shelter for homeless teens. When her mother became pregnant with Autumn, she dropped out of her Indiana high school. She and Steve moved to Florida hoping to find work. Steve found a job in construction, and they tried to save for a place to live. But in Fort Lauderdale, as in most other areas, rents are high. They needed to save enough money to pay for the first and last months' rent, a security deposit, and an electric-service deposit—nearly $2,000 in all. "It might as well be a million," a Covenant staff member told the *Christian Science Monitor.* With no money, Autumn's mother could not afford prenatal care. A doctor's advice is essential to guide young mothers in the proper diet to guard against birth defects. When Autumn's mother went into labor with Autumn, she just appeared at the Broward General Medical Center and said, "I'm here. Help me." Autumn was born homeless.[6]

The homelessness of all of the children cited above is the consequence of poverty. While some kids live homeless because they have run away, runaways have always been a problem. There have always been families in which children suffer abuse so intolerable that the streets offer the only possible alternative. Some kids are what we have come to call "throw-

The saddest victims of homelessness are the children. Three-year-old Damian lives with his mother in an abandoned building on the Lower East Side in New York City. At the time this photo was taken, there was no running water or gas hookup in the building.

aways"—children forced to leave their homes because they were not wanted or because they caused problems their family could no longer handle. Some kids have wandered away—primarily because of drug or alcohol abuse. But today, the number of kids who are homeless because their parents cannot find affordable housing, kids who have families that struggle to stay together despite the odds against them, is growing. The New York City Commission on the Year 2000 predicts that one in every seven of that city's residents—over one million family members—will either be doubled up with other families or living homeless by the end of the nineties. A study funded by the U.S. Congress maintains that nineteen million Americans across the United States will be homeless by the year 2003. Many of them will be children.[7] According to the National Coalition for the Homeless, in 1989 three-fourths of the newly homeless in the United States were families with children.[8]

DEFINING HOMELESSNESS

Homelessness is the extreme consequence of poverty. People who do not have the money to buy the barest essentials—food, clothing, and shelter—whether they work or not, are people living in poverty. It limits the kind and amount of food families eat. It limits the quantity and quality of the clothing they wear. It restricts people to houses and apartments few others would want. It sets up boundaries between those who have and those who don't. It bridles a person with problems wealthier people never have—how to provide a nutritious diet, for example, or how to get help for a sick child. Poverty is a constraint that keeps people down; it controls them by creating obstacles they often cannot overcome. It dampers their energy, it dulls their spirit. People living in poverty are confined people, restrained by a lack of alternatives or options.

The lack of choice created by poverty is the factor that most clearly characterizes the majority of today's homeless. They do not choose to sleep on park benches or in alleys, train stations, or subways. They have not willingly broken all ties to roots and family for the "romance" of being "on the road." They do not choose to travel from town to town to sleep beside the road or in abandoned buildings. While it is true that a small proportion of the men, and an even smaller proportion of the women and children, living on the streets are there for reasons other than poverty—alcohol and drug addiction, for example—most homeless people have no money to pay for shelter, or cannot find safe or decent housing on their limited incomes.

Most simply, homeless people lack homes. The bag lady, surrounded by her belongings, who has to sleep on a heat grate in New York City is clearly homeless. Others are not so easily categorized. Some live in tents or tumbledown shacks. Some live in cars or vans. Some people have to double up with other families to afford even the cheapest rooms. Some live temporarily with kind relatives. Others live in cheap hotels or flophouses on some nights and on the streets other nights. Some live in shelters, in welfare housing, in welfare motels and hotels, in missions, in school gyms, or in barracks set up for the homeless. For a time, they have a roof over their heads, even if, in many cases, that roof is provided only at night. Many shelters require homeless people to leave in the morning; they must return to the streets to wait for the shelter to reopen at night. Many people living in shelters or welfare hotels never know how long their stay will be or whether they will be told to leave on a moment's notice. Many who could stay at shelters stay on the streets rather than take the risk of being robbed or assaulted while asleep at shelters.

Homeless people not only lack choices, they live their lives in a state of transition, of impermanence, over which they have no control. The transience, or temporariness, of homelessness also makes its definition difficult. About one-fourth to one-third of all homeless people are what experts call chronically, or permanently homeless. The majority are not. They are among the group called the episodically homeless—people who find shelter for a time, then become homeless again in a cycle that can repeat itself many times. The most recent numbers of homeless people, however, are homeless for the first time. What will become of them, whether they will become chronically or episodically homeless in the next few years, cannot be predicted.[9]

THE EXTENT OF HOMELESSNESS

From January to April 1990, the 1990 census was in the news. Radio and television broadcasters stressed how important it was that *everyone* be counted. Newspapers emphasized that census takers were not out to capture illegal aliens or criminals, but merely trying to get an accurate count of everyone living in the United States. All of the media urged homeless people to assist the census takers in counting everyone, so that the extent of the homeless problem could be proven.

Toward that end, the Bureau of the Census took great pains to train and schedule census takers so that on a given series of evenings, all of the people sleeping in abandoned buildings, alleys, train stations, camps, and shelters would be counted. An impossible task, most agreed. Many of the homeless have learned to avoid government officials at all costs. Many are mentally ill—hostile or frightened people to whom the rationale of being counted makes no sense. Many are living doubled, tripled, or quadrupled up in illegal apartments and condemned buildings or in secret places they've chosen because finding them is nearly impossible. Many are in cars or vans parked in inconspicuous places, sleeping one night here, another there.

Whether the census takers were able to get an accurate count has yet to be judged. The results of the 1990 census will not be public until sometime in 1991. Yet most experts agree that the chances are slim, at best, that the Census Bureau attained its goal.

Getting an accurate count of the homeless in the United States for any given night, week, month, or year is as elusive a task as counting the grains of sand washed in by the tide. The most cautious and conservative studies estimate that approximately 200,000 adults used shelters and soup kitchens in U.S. cities across the nation in a typical week in March 1987.[10] The study did not include homeless children or adults who did not use shelters or kitchens, or homeless people of all ages living in smaller cities and towns with less than 100,000 people. On the other hand, estimates from groups that advocate for the homeless, such as the National Coalition for the Homeless, are much higher—possibly three million, according to one account. While everyone realizes that no count could ever include all homeless people living in every area every night of every year, those who advocate for the homeless charge that the government's estimates are purposely low and inaccurate, that the government's intention is to minimize the problem because it does not want to deal with it. The government, on the other hand, maintains that those who advocate for the homeless inflate their numbers to make the problem seem more serious than it is. In this way, they can put more pressure on the public to do something to remedy the situation. Both sides have spent a great deal of time and money to obtain the statistics necessary to support their claims, but a universally accepted count has yet to be taken.

The only thing almost everyone agrees with is that the number of homeless people is increasing. In 1986, the U.S. Conference of Mayors study indicated that in twenty-two of the twenty-five cities that participated, homelessness was a growing problem.[11] In 1987, the *Washington Post* reported a 500 percent increase of homeless families in one year, with a seven-year public housing waiting list of 12,000 people.[12] The U.S. General Accounting Office (GAO) estimates an annual growth of homelessness of between 10 and 38 percent.[13]

In addition, many more people are potentially homeless. They are the borderline homeless living in substandard or marginal homes on poverty-level incomes. "The potential homelessness problem in contemporary America . . . is many times worse than the actual problem being confronted today," Professor James D. Wright of Tulane University states. For many people teetering on the brink, the slightest change in their condition—a layoff, an illness, the loss of a spouse, an increase in rent, an urban renewal project that tears down their apartment building, a change in the value of the dollar, any of a hundred variables—could send them plummeting into homelessness.

THE HISTORY OF HOMELESSNESS IN THE UNITED STATES

The number of people who are homeless is not the only thing that has changed over the last several decades. Homeless people today are far different than they were before.

Homelessness in the United States dates back to earliest colonial times. In colonial Massachusetts, the "wandering poor" could receive poor relief, food and shelter, if they remained in a town for more than three months. Times were hard for everyone, and to survive all knew that they had to stick together. In the earliest communities, the prosperous and the poor lived together on the same street. But for a few differences in the size of houses or simple luxuries such as leaded-glass windows, the rich and the poor looked and lived the same. But as the years passed, and the numbers of poor and homeless grew, the rich separated themselves by moving elsewhere. The old sense of community died. The amount of money needed for poor relief increased, and so did the number of people needing it. To control their numbers and keep costs down, some towns hired agents who went from door to door to locate strangers. Once found, their names and past addresses were reviewed by the courts, after which they could be "warned out" or told to leave town.[14] Sometimes, instead of being told to leave, the poor were "bound out," forced to work for wealthier families that needed servants or hired hands. Between 28 percent and 68 percent of those warned out or bound out were two-parent families.[15] This practice lasted until it was abolished by law in 1794.

By the early 1800s, the poorhouse or almshouse replaced poor relief and became the source of shelter for homeless poor people. It didn't work. To have shelter, those in the almshouse were forced to work long hours farming, sewing, and cooking. Their diet and health were neglected. Four-fifths of them remained on the public rolls their whole lifetimes.[16] By midcentury, almshouses were replaced by settlement houses run by philanthropists and advocates for the poor like Jane Addams. By 1914, Boston's settlement houses numbered thirty-three. There, the poor found nurseries for working mothers, after-school clubs for boys, training for jobs, and classes in literacy. Settlement workers focused on impoverished families and helped those families get a new start in life.

Henry Morgan, the originator of Morgan Memorial Goodwill Industries, also worked out of Boston at this time. He began night schools for boys who worked during the day and free vocational training. His successor, Edgar Helms, turned Goodwill Industries into a model program that converted every dollars' worth of donated goods into five dollars in benefits for the needy. According to Kathleen Hirsch, author of *Songs from the Alley,* Goodwill Industries produced the equivalent of $25 million in wages for the unemployed and homeless during the depression of the 1930s, the worst, most severe time of economic hardship in United States history. But on the heels of the Depression, the government began taking over the job of caring for the poor, the elderly, and the disabled with Social Security, a legal minimum wage, the creation of public housing, and federal jobs programs. The function of organizations such as the Goodwill, the Salvation Army, settlement houses, and church-sponsored centers had been replaced by the government.

While fighting poverty and integrating the poor into mainstream society has long been a problem, the plight of homeless families, and therefore of homeless children, has only recently become an issue. When the depression ended with World War II, employable men were drafted into the armed services to fight the war, and women took their places on the assembly line. Even after the soldiers returned home in the mid-1940s, the United States economy was expanding, creating new job opportunities and a sense of growth and well-being nationwide. While homeless poor families most certainly existed during the '50s and '60s, very little was written about them. As far as the American public was concerned, the homeless were "hobos" riding the rails and living in camps alongside the tracks or they were old "skid row bums," alcoholics who had

There have always been poor and homeless people. This sketch made in 1889 shows an officer on watch along the riverfront in New York City.

chosen the bottle over job, family, and personal pride.[17]

THE CHARACTERISTICS OF TODAY'S HOMELESS

In some ways, that perception was not completely wrong. According to Professor James D. Wright in his article "Address Unknown: Homelessness in Contemporary America," a review of the medical records of the health clinic at the New York City Men's Shelter in the late sixties and early seventies shows that half of all homeless men were white, half were drug or alcohol abusers, and their average age was forty-four. In *Without Shelter* by Peter Rossi, a 1958 study in Chicago indicated that of all homeless people, only about a hundred were actually sleeping on the streets. The rest were able to find shelter in flophouses and cheap hotels, most of which no longer exist today.

Professor Wright states that the homeless are different now. Only 15 percent are white. Twenty-eight percent are drug or alcohol abusers, and their average age has dropped to thirty-six. Rossi's study shows that while the literally hopeless population in Chicago is estimated at about 3,000, nearly half actually sleep on the streets.[18] Not only has the race, ethnic background, and age of the typical homeless person changed, but that person is facing a much bleaker lifestyle than did his counterpart of two to three decades ago.

While women comprised only 3 percent of the homeless population in the 1958 Chicago study, one out of every four homeless people today is female. Females and children comprise between one-third and two-fifths of all homeless people. If eighty people were a representative sample of all of the homeless, according to Professor Wright, twelve of them would be children or teenagers under nineteen years of age. Another eighteen to nineteen of the group would be adult women. Together the two groups' members would total thirty of the original eighty people. Of the fifty men remaining, nearly twenty would either be elderly or veterans of the U.S. armed services, leaving three-eighths, or thirty remaining. Ten of those thirty would be disabled by mental illness and two by physical handicaps, making them incapable of work. Of the remaining eighteen, more than half would be working at least some of the time, but still unable to find affordable housing. Of those not working, at least half would be looking for work. Of the original eighty, only 2.5 would have no reason for homelessness, other than perhaps a reluctance to work or a lack of responsibility.[19]

These statistics are interesting for two reasons: 1) they show that the current problem of homelessness in the United States is not a result of a growing shiftlessness or laziness of its people, but most often the consequence of factors over which the homeless have no control, and 2) while it is relatively easy to ignore hobos and winos, it is quite another thing to ignore children, single mothers, victims of mental illness and war, and men who would rather work, if only jobs were available.

Except for a small percentage, the vast majority of the homeless could and would live differently had they the chance to do so. And the group for whom the least number of options exists is the group that statistically is growing faster than any other. According to Jonathan Kozol in *Rachel and Her Children,* child poverty has increased 50 percent since the late 1960s. It affects one of every three children under the age of six, one-third of all children, fully one-half of all black children,[20] and 14 million children in all.[21] While many of these children are not literally homeless, their parent or parents earn below the federal poverty level, which is currently $9,435 for a family of three.[22]

That means they are easily in jeopardy of becoming homeless at any given time. In New York City, 18,000 parents and children from 5,000 families are actually homeless, living in shelters. In some parts of Massachusetts, 90 to 95 percent of all homeless persons are family members, parents with children. While the Committee on Health Care for Homeless People of the National Academy of Sciences has reported that 100,000 children under the age of eighteen are homeless,[23] Kozol insists that almost five times that many children are homeless in America. "If all of them were gathered in one city, they would represent a larger population than that of Atlanta, Denver, or St. Louis."[24]

Enough children to fill a city. Enough families to fill several cities. They constitute what has come to be known as "the new homeless," because they no longer fit the popular old stereotype of the vagrant or hobo. Their numbers are growing at such a rate that it is becoming increasingly more difficult to ignore them or their misery.

Many groups concerned about the growth of homeless families and homelessness in general have begun to piece together a picture of this segment of impoverished American society. Their findings, however, do not always coincide with the findings of other studies. According to many reports, the majority of these families have until only recently been self-reliant, able to fend for themselves without the aid of welfare. They indicate the "new homeless" are uncomfortably similar to the average American. As the president of the Texas Gulf Coast United Way told the Houston, Texas *Chronicle,* one of the reasons the families of these children have come to be called "the new homeless" is because prior to coming for help, they "have never even seen a shelter." Democratic Representative Charles Schumer of New York state has said that

"The vast majority of homeless are like you and me; they simply cannot afford housing."[25] When NBC's Tom Brokaw interviewed some of rural Iowa's homeless families in 1988, he told viewers the homeless are "people you know."[26] They are so much like every other American that author Gay Talese wrote in *New York Magazine* ". . . identifying [them] visually is often impossible. Increasingly, the victims [of urban destitution and despair] in our streets are looking like the rest of us."[27]

Whether the members of homeless families look startlingly like the people next door or people you know may or may not be true. Other statistics about them paint a slightly different picture. According to Jonathan Kozol, the typical homeless family consists of one parent, average age twenty-seven, raising two to three children whose ages average six.[28] *U.S. News & World Report* adds that most homeless parents are either black or Hispanic single women. Few have job experience, or if they have worked, they have been unemployed an average of four years. *Society* magazine reports that most of these families have been driven to homelessness by causes such as illness, divorce, desertion, eviction, and foreclosure,[29] while *U.S. News & World Report* states the cause of their homelessness most likely to be domestic violence—wife battering or child abuse.[30]

THE IMPORTANCE OF THE HOMELESS PROBLEM

While it may be true that the average homeless family is not precisely like the family next door, the statistics on these families, their race or ethnic origins, the ages of parents and children, the obstacles they have faced, and the kinds of problems they must solve if they are to achieve independence, are important. They indicate a trend in our society. They prove without question that something is wrong with the way things are happening in our culture. They establish who is most adversely affected and how. Most importantly, however, the statistics clearly reveal that increasingly large numbers of children are growing up in what can only be described as desperate circumstances. Those circumstances will almost definitely have dire effects on their futures. It will not be long before society as a whole must face the consequences of their deprivation.

U.S. News & World Report calls them "America's investment in misery," the *Christian Science Monitor,* a new "bio-underclass," and the Supplemental Statement to the Institute of Medicine's report, "a national disgrace that must be treated with the urgency that such a situation demands . . . an outrage, a national scandal." They are children who hang about their parents' knees while they wait in welfare agencies, children who line up in soup kitchens for their food. They play in abandoned buildings, littered lots, beneath bridges, and in makeshift urban campgrounds. Some seldom sleep, and when they do, their beds are the backseats of cars, the floors of tents, or plastic sheets spread beneath crates and boxes. Some sleep in flophouses, others in shelters run by public and private agencies.

Because they and their parents are powerless to make choices, without the options money provides, they are "uneducated, unhealthy, and angry at society." "It is hard to remember that this is America, not Calcutta," Kay McChesney, a sociologist, told *U.S. News & World Report.* Their poverty and, therefore, their plight is not very different from the poverty of the great masses of poor in underdeveloped countries. According to *Society* magazine, while homelessness is widespread in those countries, "relative to our history and our national expectation, [it] strikes a shockingly discordant note."

How these growing numbers of children came to be homeless, what their lives are like, how they live by day and where they sleep at night, the obstacles they face to survive, to obtain an education, and to remain healthy is the subject of this book. It is also a book about the breakdown of the American dream—the dream that all people can be equal and can have an even chance with all others of attaining their goals. Should society continue in its present direction, for those unfortunates living in poverty and for the society that has created them, the future may someday be called the American nightmare.

CHAPTER 2
WITHOUT SHELTER

In Westchester County, less than an hour from New York City, the 3,000-acre (1214-hectare) Rockefeller estate sprawls green and luxurious just down the road from the Elmsford Motor Lodge, where homeless children pile their clothes in corners and an entire family tries to live in rooms designed for two to spend a night. Nearby, on Route 287, gigantic corporate parks surround the headquarters of some of the richest companies in the country—Texaco, Pepsico, and International Paper.[1] In this area, Brad Kessler wrote in *The Nation,* the average house sells for $300,000; the average family income is $40,000 a year. The residents, many of them executives, can buy their children designer clothes and take yearly jaunts to ski resorts and Bahamian beaches. Their children soon learn that success is the password—that success, money, acceptance, and power are proper goals if one is to live well. Yet while Westchester children are among the wealthiest children in the nation, Westchester has more homeless persons per capita than any other place in the nation.[2]

On Fifth Avenue in nearby New York City, Jacqueline Onassis, widow of the late President John F. Kennedy, and other equally powerful and wealthy people, live in apartments that can cost as much as six million dollars. Myron Magnet, writing for *Fortune* magazine, describes the view from their windows, if they look down. It is of tattered homeless sleeping among "bundles turned dead grey by dirt and wear."[3] There, the homeless wait in lines for a meal while shoppers hurry by, their bags rich and heavy with luxuries. There also, poor children huddle against the cold in doorways to some of the wealthiest buildings and sleep on park benches meant for afternoon strollers.

If it is true that where we live and where we are from are sources of our identity, today's wandering homeless children and their families form an anonymous army that defies comprehension. To most of society, they are mysteries, without names or individual stories. Most of society is dumbfounded by the size and scope of the homelessness problem, especially the numbers of homeless mothers and children. "What happened to these families?" they ask. "Why are they homeless?" "Why are they sleeping all over the streets?" The source of the problem or a reasonable quick solution has so far eluded our government and private organizations concerned with their welfare. As a result, society has grown impatient with the homeless—not impatient with the government's lack of effective problem solving, but impatient with the *victims* of poor problem solving, the homeless. Gertrude Himmelfarb, author of *The Idea of Poverty,* characterized the public attitude: "We're beginning to feel they're permanent, and they demoralize the whole society."[4]

Nowhere has society's impatience become more apparent than at historic Grand Central Station in New York City. There, arriving and departing commuters must run what one reporter dubbed "a gauntlet" of beggars and panhandlers, avoiding the slightest eye contact with the homeless poor who coil in corners or stretch out on plastic bags in the corridors. They are everywhere, the commuters complain, prowling about, looking for an easy touch, an unwary tourist quick to toss a few coins rather than be accosted by dirty, ragged people.

Commuter complaints have led authorities to crack down on the poor taking shelter at Grand Central Station. The building is now closed from 2 A.M. until the morning rush hours. Security forces hustle the homeless out, checking every nook and cranny they can, rousting those sleeping there. Many people are agitating for new laws against panhandling, an activity now protected by the First Amendment to the Constitution, the right to freedom of speech. Others who must walk the gauntlet to reach their trains or subways have become colder, much more callous with the beggars. "Get a job," they now hiss, while a few years ago, they wanted to help. A few years ago, concerned citizens asked, "What can we do for these people?" Today, with the numbers of homeless increasing, and with few, if any, systems working to change the trend, the question is much more likely to be, "What are we going to do about these people?"

What the government has done so far about the people too poor to afford decent, safe, respectable housing is to create a legion of systems and provisions for shelter that have done little to reverse the growth of homelessness or even improve the quality of life for the homeless. The problem, of course, is that the homeless have created a philosophical dilemma for the United States. On the one hand, the framers of our Constitution did not design a welfare state, a government that provides food and shelter for its people. The idea of self-sufficiency, the ability to care for oneself, is almost as basic to United States principles as are the ideas of freedom and democracy. On the other hand, the United States is one of the richest countries in the world and has always prided itself on the standard of living its people have achieved. Unfortunately, how much or how little the government should or should not do for homeless people is not always clear. While United States citizens, lawmakers, politicians, and leaders struggle to define the role of government in providing for the welfare of its citizens, however, the children of poor parents without homes struggle daily to survive.

PRIVATE HOUSING

About two-thirds of all the children and their families who are living at or below poverty level make their homes in buildings owned by private citizens or else they go homeless.[5] Only one in every three families lives in federally assisted housing because the waiting lists are so long or because, like Rosie Slusher and her children, parents so fear conditions in the projects that they choose to live homeless rather than take any more chances. Decent private housing for a family like Ms. Slusher's that is affordable—costing less than $250 a month—is impossible to find. Filthy, substandard, unsafe housing for less than $250 a month exists, but it is also becoming harder to find.

Poor kids growing up in substandard housing are always vulnerable and endangered. They are not much better off than homeless kids, except that temporarily, at least, they do have a "place." But while they may have a place, they are living in marginal housing, on the brink of homelessness should authorities clamp down on illegal apartments and condemn unsafe buildings, or should a fire, loss of parent's income, or illness destroy their ability to pay. Substandard housing is any housing that does not meet basic

Whether the issue is rural or urban conditions, the major problem facing the country's poverty-stricken population is the lack of decent housing.

safety and sanitary codes. Substandard housing can be anything from garages, tool sheds, and chicken coops to dilapidated and unsafe tenements. The Los Angeles *Times* reports that an estimated 200,000 people, most of them parents and children, are currently renting some 42,000 garages in the city. Yolanda Gonzalez's daughter, husband, and granddaughter live with her in one such garage. The baby plays on the linoleum floor, while around her exposed electrical wires run along the unfinished walls. Such "garage-apartments" cost anywhere from $200 to $600 a month to rent. Even worse are the *colonias* that are spreading throughout the lower Rio Grande valley in Texas. Colonias are rural subdivisions that are the poorest in the United States. There, another (unrelated) Gonzalez family, ten of them children, live in a "cramped, dark and drafty three-room shack." The homes in "the valley" have no heat or sewers. Rain floods the roads and yards with raw sewage through which the children must wade to get to school. A quarter of a million people live in the valley, where unemployment has been running 50 percent and disease is rampant. Roberto Costilla's mother, unable to pay the developer's water-supply bill, rose every morning to fetch and haul eight 10-gallon buckets from a neighbor's house so that her family could have water to wash with and drink. When Roberto and then his father developed strange open sores on their faces and arms, the Costillos learned they had been drinking water contaminated with bodily wastes.[6]

While some poor families live in rural shacks, others live in tenements that are tinderboxes, that could explode into fire with the strike of a match. They are crowded together in crumbling rooms that often have no provision for cooking. Many times the plumbing does not work, and heat invariably goes off for days during the coldest months of the year. Tenements are often rat, roach, and lice infested, filthy and toxic, electrically unsafe and unprotected by fire alarms or sprinkler systems. In short, private-sector housing in the price range of America's poor is an American shame. Yet poor people, those working as well as those on welfare, are finding it increasingly difficult to find even *that* for shelter.

Several factors have contributed to make the housing situation so impossible for poor families. Often poor people are forced to move from substandard buildings that are then torn down and replaced with new, usually middle- or upper-income apartments. This process is called "gentrification," after the word "gentry," meaning those of good breeding. So common is the practice in Newark, New Jersey, for instance, that city councilman Donald Tucker told *Newsweek* "the city is running poor people out of town." By displacing the poor and replacing them with wealthier people, the gentrification of entire neighborhoods that once housed city poor has severely reduced the number of affordable apartments.

Sometimes buildings have been torched by arsonists, frequently for the healthy insurance settlement the fire will bring or to save the cost of their demolition. Other times, buildings have been converted to coops or condominiums, which the poor cannot afford to buy. At the same time, the government has cut back the funds and incentives it once offered to builders to construct or rehabilitate low-income housing; these funds have dropped from $32 billion in 1975 to $9 billion today.[7] While the number of affordable housing units lessens, however, the number of families desperate for a home has increased. The National Low-Income Housing Coalition claims that one million additional units are needed now, and that number is expected to grow substantially during the 1990s.[8] Unfortunately, once landlords recognized that the demand for their units was spiraling despite their condition, they raised the rents. For the poor, many of them living on welfare, working for minimum wages, or retired on limited Social Security payments, the rise in housing costs was disastrous. According to Jonathan Kozol, rent allowances set by the city for those on welfare in New York, for example, remained frozen for ten years at their 1975 level. Yet actual rent costs doubled and tripled. The minimum wage for those trying to support their families climbed slowly in comparison to the cost of housing, increasing the gap between the cash a working family earned and the amount they had to pay for shelter. Retired and single adults living in SRO's (single-room occupancy hotels) on their meager Social Security checks found themselves evicted when the owners sold to developers or razed the buildings to erect expensive high-rise office or apartment buildings.

Consider the two young children whose mother works forty hours a week for $3.35 an hour at a local fast-food restaurant in Houston, Texas. According to the Star of Hope Mission, each month she earns $536.00. By the time she buys her family food, which costs at least $50 a week or $200 a month; buys bus tokens to get to and from work, which costs $25 a month; pays her income tax and Social Security withholding tax, which total $94.54; she has about $216 left to pay for housing—if she can find it. And even if she does find something, which today is unlikely, she has no money left for child care, for a doctor or medicine if any of the children get sick, or for buying and laundering clothing.[9]

According to Jonathan Kozol, families whose rent or mortgage costs exceed 50 percent of their monthly income are families literally on the brink of becoming homeless.[10] In the United States, over 6 million households pay more than half of their income for rent.

These family members were forced to camp out in a park when they lost their home. Too many Americans have had to face similar dire circumstances.

Four million, seven hundred thousand pay 60 percent or more. Two million pay over half their income for mortgage interest. "Combining these households with those who are doubled up (living two families or more to a unit)," Kozol states, "it appears that well above 10 million families may be living near the edge of homelessness in the U.S." "Even people living out in the suburbs are often just one or two paychecks away from disaster,"[11] one person told *Christianity Today.*

When parents no longer have enough money to cover expenses, housing is usually the first thing to go, most experts agree.[12] The sum owed for rent or for a mortgage payment is probably the only debt that must always be paid on the first day of each month. It is also the largest of the family's monthly expenses, and it cannot be divided into smaller, more manageable sums. Nor can it be late. A family can scrimp on food, eating less expensive cuts of meat or smaller portions. It can put off buying shoes, and often will delay seeking medical help. But the first of each month rolls around with cruel regularity. And while a landlord might wait a week or even longer for payment, the rental debt keeps growing larger and more impossible with every passing day.

THE NEXT STEP

Once the decision is made that, for a while at least, housing is no longer affordable, families have few alternatives. In suburban and rural areas, many people who lose their homes decide to camp out. When the Conway family of Springfield, Virginia, left their home in 1987, they had only $1,700 of their savings left. They sold most of their furniture in a tag sale, packed the rest in a trailer, and moved to the Burke Lake campground Mrs. Conway had visited when she was younger. The Conways thought that they could easily pay the $9 per night campground fee, rebuild their savings, and wait until the strike that had put Mr. Conway out of work ended. But camping was neither easy, nor did it allow the Conways to save. Mrs. Conway had to send her two oldest boys from a previous marriage to their father in Florida. "You don't even have a bathroom or hot water," Mrs. Conway told Miriam Van Scott of *Good Housekeeping* magazine. "And the public schools won't enroll kids from the camp because they don't have a permanent address . . . No one wanted to help. Social Service spent most of the time trying to prove that we didn't exist. The county said it was a migrant-worker issue . . ."[13]

While some families fight to maintain a shred of decency as "campers," others, not so lucky, make their cars their homes. Five thousand people live in their cars in the San Fernando Valley of California alone. They park in public parking lots, along side roads, and in broken-down areas. In California, Municipal Code 85.02 forbids using a car as a residence, but for some homeless poor, like Crissy Damm and her family, no other choices exist. When Anne Fadiman of *Life* magazine lived with one homeless family for a week, she was witness to the discomfort and frustration families experience living out of their cars: "Do I have to lie on the bump in the floor?" Crissy asked her mother Linda. Linda, folded onto the backseat, snapped, "I've made up your bed, and you're gonna sleep in it."[14]

While "homeless families are more likely to be hidden from the public eye, living marginally from night to night in shelters, welfare hotels and cars," Anne Fadiman wrote in *Life,* youngsters—teenagers trying to make it on their own—are more likely to live on the streets. According to the 1989 UNICEF annual report, 100 million children live on the streets of the world's big cities.[15] Some maintain family connections but work the streets to help their families make ends meet. Some live on the streets, seeking food, shelter and a social bond among other street children while still maintaining some family ties. Some have been abandoned by their families and live completely on their own. Many of the homeless children in the United States are runaways and throwaways. They are most often escaping intolerable conditions at home. Physical or sexual abuse is the common reason for teenagers to strike out on their own. The life they find is often as bad or worse than what they left. In *Newsweek,* Pete Axthelm described a typical homeless teen hanging out on a street corner:

> *At the corner of Fern, a lanky youth named Bill is leaning against a wire fence. His seconds have turned into days. Beneath filthy blond hair, his acned face is gaunt. He is shaking from shoulders to knees. He wears a wool jacket, possibly a relic of innocent tourist days, with a souvenir patch that reads, "San Diego Aeronautics Hall of Fame." It is smeared with blood. Blood is also caked between all his fingers, where he has been injecting speed.*[16]

Without the skills and social values they need to survive, many homeless teens turn to crime, drugs, and prostitution. Wendell says,

> *I figured it would be fun to be a hustler. I'd seen guys in movies, living by their wits. I figured I could handle the sex part all right and stay in charge of things. It was OK, too, for one summer. . . . And then I found out that I wasn't in charge of anything. The first time I had to hustle, I was as trapped as anyone out here. My life is ruined. And like the rest, I can't get out of the fast lane.*[17]

TAKING SHELTER

While there are many ways to take shelter when a family or child becomes homeless, few of them are easy and many are degrading. In New York City, homeless families must file into one of the many Income Maintenance Centers scattered throughout the city. There the children wait, hanging about their parent's knees or sleeping curled up on the uncomfortable metal chairs or on the dusty floor for countless hours while their parent waits for one of the workers to find them shelter. If no shelter is available before evening, a family must go to an Emergency Assistance Unit (EAU), which is always open, even on weekends. The EAU will assign the family to one of two kinds of places—either a barracks shelter or an emergency welfare hotel. Overtired, and having already been shunted here and there throughout the day, on first entering a barracks shelter, the family must wonder how things could possibly be worse. According to the *New York Times:*

> *Inside the shelters, where as many as two dozen families sleep in vast rooms, parents and children press their cots together so they can have more than the usual three feet between their beds and the next family. . . . Families have learned to place a crib at the end of a row of beds and then drape a blanket on its outer edge to form a sort of barrier. It is a small, largely futile gesture, but one that almost everyone makes.*[18]

Privacy is not possible in the barracks shelters. What one mother says to another is heard by everyone around. The noise intensifies as the children play, running around their beds, shouting to other children.

Barracks shelters are not a very pleasant option for many homeless people. The lack of privacy and tight quarters can lead to even greater tension and conflict for people who already have enough hardship in their lives.

The walls echo. At night, a crying child will wake everyone, including other children. Staggering to the bathroom, still half asleep, requires winding one's way through a sea of cots. It is impossible to dress or use the lavatory in private. It is life in a fishbowl, and it can create a terrible strain on everyone in the family. With so many watching eyes and listening ears, it is impossible to iron out differences or voice frustrations. One family that broke up after a three-month stay in a Colorado shelter told *U.S. News & World Report:* "It was the loss of communication more than anything."[19] The intimacies that often bond families must also be postponed. One mother told the *Houston Chronicle* the "hard thing is not being able to sleep with my husband. He sleeps up there—and sometimes at night he dangles his hand down and we just hold hands."[20]

Washington D.C. homeless shelters described by local television reporter Jack Cloherty not only allowed no privacy, but had little else as well:

> *Rats, scabies, lice, and urine-soaked mattresses are abundant at the [Pierce and Blair] shelters. Showers, sheets, towels, toilet seats and toilet paper are not. Pierce offers four showers . . . Blair . . . offers none.*[21]

The *Washington Post* reports that the number of homeless families seeking emergency shelter in that city increased more than 500 percent in 1989. Pushed to the limit, the city placed thirty-nine homeless children and their parents in a rooming house for prostitutes known as the Annex:

> *In the Annex, mothers put milk on the windowsill to keep it cold. Families are confronted with*

drug paraphernalia in shared restrooms and children mingle with prostitutes and clients. . . . The owner of the rooming house describes it as unfit for children. "This is a pigpen," he told a Post *reporter. But the city keeps the children in the pigpen for almost a year.*[22]

The prostitutes and their clients may be the worst problem, but they are not the only one. Exit signs light locked doors. Smoke detectors are broken. Window sash cords are cut, their ends stolen by drug users to tie off their arms.[23]

Not all shelters are terrible. Many of them, most often those run privately by churches and civic groups, are clean. The volunteers in these shelters offer not only blankets and beds but kindness and respect as well. But they are not the norm, and the effect of most shelters on children and their parents is divisive and degrading. The lack of privacy and the sense of being warehoused tend to diminish an already weak sense of self-esteem. Yet the parents of kids without homes try hard to make their children feel like other, more fortunate kids:

Most of the women are dressed neatly, and some of the kids are in adorable get-ups: Bows in hair and party shoes for the girls, superhero jackets and team ballcaps for the boys. Obviously, many of these people are using their meager means for the right things; given more sustenance, most of them would only do more of the same . . . for the Belmont families, it seems that housing would be a big part of the answer.[24]

Some young children are dropped off at baby-sitters and even fewer at federally run preschools, and some of the older children go to school, but others remain with their parents each morning as they return to the welfare center. They must do this in cities like New York City because their change of address to the shelter must be recorded or they can lose welfare benefits. Usually their stay in the barracks shelter has been so uncomfortable that everyone is cranky for lack of sleep and because of the stress of living in a crowd. All are hoping that the EAU worker will find them a better place, hopefully a short-term hotel, where they can have a room to themselves, perhaps even their own bathroom, and some family privacy. At a short-term hotel, the family may be able to spend a few days before once again going back to the EAU for a new assignment. Each time they return to the EAU, parents and children ask for a less temporary assignment, where the children can go to school, begin to make some regular friends, and feel more at home. According to Jonathan Kozol, that hope is usually dashed. According to a study by the New York City Council, "Instead, the homeless family often must stay at another short-term hotel for a few days before returning to the EAU. This cycle can continue for months, even years."[25] The family can be placed anywhere in the city, for any amount of time, without rhyme or reason. Mothers and children are shuttled about like "human pinballs"[26] in a game over which no one seems to have any control and in which the major players seem to have less concern for the people on the game board than they would for plastic pieces.

Once a family does attain placement in a long-term hotel, however, their problems are far from over. Of the sixty or more welfare hotels in New York City, eleven housed more than 100 families and at least three contained 1,000 families by the end of 1986.[27] One hotel, at Eighth Avenue and 43rd Street, has peeling lead paint. The *New York Times* reports that the

Some homeless children are fortunate enough to end up in a shelter like this one in New Jersey. These well-dressed, well-cared-for children represent only a small minority of the homeless children in the United States.

Legal Aid Society has threatened the city with a lawsuit. "The conditions are worse here than at any other welfare hotel. Literally every room in the facility has unlawful levels of lead paint." At the hotel, inspectors found garbage that had accumulated for three weeks, fire extinguishers kept out of reach in the basement, and windows that lacked guards. In addition, the number of security men had been cut to save costs—in spite of the fact that muggings in the hallways and elevators had increased.[28] The New York *Daily News* also reported that residents were complaining about fires being set and guns stored and traded illegally on the premises.

In welfare hotels, the rooms are almost always in battered condition. In the typical two-room unit Jonathan Kozol observed—a unit that was costing the city $3,000 a month to rent—the bathroom walls were crumbling, the tiles were cracked or missing, and the toilet was broken. The entire room reeked, and a pan, placed strategically on the floor, caught something dripping regularly from the ceiling plaster.[29]

While welfare housing in cities like New York may be burdened to the breaking point, suburban emergency housing is not much better. In suburban and rural areas, once prosperous motels that have fallen on hard times serve the same role as New York City's welfare hotels. In Burbank, California, 90 percent of the Scott Motel's residents are homeless people. According to *Life* magazine, the Scott is preferred because, "unlike the proprietors of other local motels, its owners do not complain that their guests are wasting electricity if they leave the lights on all night to keep the cockroaches from crawling on their beds."[30] In Westchester County, New York, the forty or more motels that have been converted to welfare units can house only one-fifth of its homeless population. The chances of a family's being placed near home, family, or roots are rather slim. More often than not, Westchester officials will pick a motel as far away as the Pennsylvania border or shuttle a family up to Poughkeepsie or Newburgh, New York. Those housed in these distant areas face a two-hour cab ride if the children want to remain in Westchester's schools, a ride that will cost the county $220 round-trip. Homeless parents who have a job in Westchester will more than likely have to give it up, because the county will not pay for their transportation to and from work.[31]

As with the city hotels, welfare motels are rife with crime and drugs. "People who live in the Elmsford Motor Lodge [in Westchester County, New York] . . . say more than 80 percent of the residents use crack," reports Brad Kessler in the *Nation.* Most begin their addiction *after* arriving, one resident told him. "You get people coming in here that are so nice at the beginning, but by the time they leave here, they're drug addicts or they're so bitter because this place just makes them crazy."[32]

In the Norwalk-Westport Motel in Connecticut, Barbara Jones and her three boys, and fourteen other families on public assistance, each cram their belongings into one-room units. "I'm hoping to land a rental through Section 8 (a federal subsidy program), but I know I'm way down on the list," she told a reporter from the *Fairpress.*[33] Meanwhile, what happens to the children shunted, crammed, dropped, and forgotten in these places of last resort?

In some cases, the children sense their isolation from mainstream society. With too many of them crowded into too few rooms, what cities and towns seem to be trying to accomplish is the warehousing of human lives. Even the motels, like the Elmsford Motor Lodge or the Parkway Motel in Westchester, are

> *located on a wooded ridge, invisible to those driving by on Tarrytown Road. The people who live*

in the motels feel they are being hidden and speak often of their isolation, of having nowhere to go, nothing to do. Placed in an alien, often hostile community, they stay inside their rooms and rarely go out. Even people who have lived in the motels for more than a year say they have little or no contact with the surrounding neighborhoods. And so the motels have become suburban ghettos, keeping the homeless to themselves . . . yet there are no kitchens or living rooms or stoves, no place, no matter how dreary or destitute, they can call home.[34]

On a commercial street like the Boston Post Road, where the Norwalk-Westport Motel is located, children can't play in a yard or ride their tricycles up and down sidewalks. In the Capitol City Inn in Washington, D.C., children either hustle quarters in the traffic, washing windows while the cars stop for lights, or play on the railroad tracks between commuter trains. In the isolated areas beside superhighways in Westchester, welfare motel children have no way to make friends or develop the kind of bond that can give them the social skills they'll need to survive in the adult world. What kind of adults will they become if the life they grow into is like Michelle's daughter's?

Michelle can pretty much deal with life in the motel, with the maids who steal her medication and the baby's stuffed animals, with the addicts who smoke crack in the bathroom upstairs and whose clouds of cocaine smoke blow down through the vents into her apartment. She can deal with doors slamming around her at all hours of the night, with having nowhere to cook a hot meal.

. . . But the bugs are another thing entirely. It's not the cockroaches that she minds so much—although she leaves the lights on at night to keep them away—it's the ants, the biting kind, the ones that crawl up the legs of her baby's crib and get to its face, its eyes, its nostrils.[35]

Finding shelter has become the preoccupation of millions of America's poor. Finding *decent* shelter has, in the last two decades, become a far-off dream. Yet despite countless hardships, those living at or below the poverty level in the United States continue to struggle to provide their children with safe shelter. The myth, of course, is that the poor are all clamoring for public assistance—to live off the dole. The fact is that only about half of all those who could qualify for social welfare—housing assistance, food stamps, disability pensions, and other welfare programs—in fact do actually apply for or receive it.[36] Getting help when a family first becomes homeless is a herculean task. Overburdened social agencies discourage those who come for help, often burying them with forms and appointments, complex requirements, and a maze of steps to be taken that are designed to deter all but the most persistent. Many families will do everything they can to avoid welfare offices, going only as a last resort.

Robert Coles, in a *Vogue* article entitled "Lost Youth," describes the parents of a ten-year-old boy and his seven-year-old sister. Their father had been hospitalized with a chronic, disabling disease. Their mother needed surgery, yet she refused to seek the state's help, trying instead to stand on her own. The children were shunted off to a friend's home, and when their mother returned, she, too, stayed with the friend until it was no longer possible. "I looked and looked for an apartment, but I didn't have the money. I had no savings. I was just getting on my feet. I was desperate—we'd be living on the street unless something happened."[37]

For those receiving aid, the actual purchasing power of every one of today's welfare dollars is worth roughly half of what it was twenty years ago.[38] To restore the quality of life welfare families had twenty years ago would literally require the government to double present welfare benefits. Twenty years ago, a welfare family could find decent housing on their welfare allotments. Yet while the Children's Defense Fund states that child poverty has increased 50 percent since 1969, according to the *New York Times,* welfare benefits to families with children have declined 35 percent.[39]

Today, the poor are caught up in a cycle that will not release them. The last and final step for Rosie Slusher and her children—the family that left the projects after one child was thrown down the stairs—or for Jessica, Christopher, and Sheina—the family that had to forsake sleep to protect the baby from rats—will probably follow months of waiting and looking for an apartment they can afford on their benefits. In the long run, the only housing they're going to find, if they're lucky, will be more of the same—depressing, deteriorating, and dangerous public housing.

The housing situation is not likely to improve in the near future. More people losing their jobs will mean more people losing their homes. In Oklahoma, Arkansas, and Texas, where both the oil and agricultural businesses are dying, farms, restaurants, stores, barbershops, and grocery stores are shutting down.[40] In rural areas of the Midwest, farmers are being shut out by the big conglomerates and by a rash of hard growing seasons. The lumber industry in Oregon, Washington, and northern Maine is suffering. The automobile industries that employ or support most of

Detroit are suffering. According to the U.S. Conference of Mayors:

> *The new poor are not being recalled to their former jobs, because their former plants are not being reopened. . . . Their temporary layoffs are from dying industries. Two million jobs in steel, textiles, and other industries, according to the AFL-CIO, have disappeared each year since 1979. Nearly half of all new jobs created from 1979 to 1985 pay poverty-level wages.*[41]

With the radical changes that have occurred in inner-city real estate, the recent trend to cut or end federal subsidies for low-income housing, and the downturn of the economy, the family that comes on hard times today faces an obstacle course of epic proportions. Few have relatives who will or can offer much help, for the extended family—the network of aunts and cousins, uncles and brothers—that used to exist as a safety net for families in trouble is also vanishing.

Not only has the extended family vanished, but housing rules and regulations abound today, many of them designed to limit the number of people living in a single unit. Thus mothers, aunts, and sisters who would otherwise offer some shelter are forbidden to do so by their own lease agreements. Such lease agreements also frequently bar children from a rental unit. This discriminatory policy has barred children from 60 percent of all housing built since 1979.[42] In addition, other governmental oversights have added to the burden of families with children. *Life* magazine cited one situation in which a federal grant subsidizing shelter fees for families expired, leading to the eviction of the Damm family.

"Where will we sleep tomorrow?" Crissy Damm asked as her mother rocked her back and forth.

"I don't want to sleep on the street. I'll be hit by a car!" Jesse Damm wailed.

Later, Mrs. Damm told them, "If I cried every time something went wrong, I'd be crying for the rest of my life."[43]

While the tears of a mother or her homeless children may not inspire government or local politicians to solve the problem of kids without homes, the economic realities should. In the Norwalk-Westport area of Connecticut, for example, the cost of a room for a family like the Damms is $50 to $60 a night, or as much as $1,860 a month at a welfare motel. For less than a third of that, a decent apartment with cooking facilities and one to two bedrooms is available. Exemplary apartments and condominiums rent for less than $1,000. Yet rather than subsidize the difference between what welfare allows for rent and the actual costs of decent housing in the area, states continue to line the pockets of motel owners at the expense of both the poor and the taxpayers who support them.[44]

In New York City, the same situation occurs on a far larger scale. The average length of stay in one of New York City's welfare hotels is thirteen months.[45] The average cost of a single month is $1,900 for a family of four, up to $3,000 for a family of six. The total cost of housing is $39,000 for an average stay, after which the problem is anything but solved. The city must continue, in most cases, to subsidize the apartment or public-housing unit a family leaving the hotel might find, or it may well find the family once again returned to the emergency housing cycle for another round.

Even if the family does not spend a year in a welfare hotel, the costs of other types of emergency shelters are far greater than what private organizations are able to provide. Barracks shelters, for example, cost $65 per night per family of four, but the additional costs for what the city calls social services and administration bring the actual cost of a barrack shelter night to $200, or as Jonathan Kozol points out, "$70,000, if projected for a year. Enough to buy a nice home."[46]

Many systems have been tried to breach the gap between rent allowances and the actual costs of apartments. "Section Eight" is a plan provided by the federal government that provides eligible applicants with a certificate that guarantees landlords government payment of a certain portion of the rent. Unfortunately, landlords prefer clients who do not need these certificates and often refuse them. The certificates are, for the most part, worthless, and if they are not used immediately, they expire. Thus a welfare family must constantly reapply for a piece of paper that, in fact, doesn't help them much at all when it comes to finding a home. The Department of Housing and Urban Development (HUD) has also created a voucher system which is designed to allow homeless families to find affordable housing by paying the difference between the 30 percent of their income they must allow for housing and the actual cost of a unit. This plan, too, has fallen far short of expectations in the tight housing market of today.[47]

In his article "Lost Youth," Robert Coles quoted the five-year-old daughter of one homeless parent who asked her mother, "How many times will we have to move until we stop?" The mother, Coles wrote, had no reply. Finally, the small girl said, "Only when we find a home can we catch our breath and be like everybody else."[48] Coles also described a sixth-grade girl living with her two sisters, her brother, and her mother in a motel room—"a 'temporary arrangement'," she said, using a phrase she had learned to know well. 'Someday, we might get a place to live, where we can stay put. . . . You're not wandering anymore. You can unpack, and discover where all you own is—the stuff you've been carrying around. You can be yourself, and not someone waiting for the time to pass until you have your own place'."[49]

Coles describes the difference between the drawings by children with homes and those by children without. He points out that in drawings by homeless children, "the eyes are tiny, the ears lacking, the mouth a mere line, the bodies quite small. In these drawings, there is no sky, no sun. Nor is there ground beneath the small feet of the mother or the almost indecipherable feet of the sister. These are people suspended in air."[50]

Suspended in air is the lot of all homeless children. If, as most psychiatrists and psychologists agree, we do define ourselves by our country, our state, our city, neighborhood, street, and home, then what we are creating today is a legion of soon-to-be-adults with no sense of self or belonging. Such childhood traumas do not disappear with age; they merely continue to plague children throughout adolescence and adulthood, altering the patterns of lives often without conscious awareness. As Anna Freud, the founder of child psychoanalysis, told Coles: "Our sense of ourselves has to do with the people, the places, the things in our lives. When children are cut loose from a particular place, when there is no reliable continuity in their lives . . . then they are not only literally homeless, they are also psychologically adrift—transients or wanderers in their minds."[51]

CHAPTER 3
STAYING ALIVE

As the United States enters the decade of the '90s, the number of people experiencing severe hardship in providing their families with the most basic essentials is dramatically increasing. Nearly a million more children between the ages of five and seventeen come from families living below the poverty level as the United States enters the nineties than at the beginning of the eighties. Fewer than nine out of every one hundred fathers or single-mother heads-of-families had incomes below the poverty level in 1980, while today, nearly twelve do. In one year, between 1984 and 1985, the number of people lining up at soup kitchens increased 28 percent.[1] Although the number of people existing under economic hardships has increased 13 percent, the number receiving food stamps has increased only slightly over 3 percent. Food stamps allow a person approximately $45 worth of edibles per month, or fifty cents a meal.[2] An orange costs approximately twenty cents. A pound of grapes costs ninety cents. A loaf of bread, on the average, costs eighty cents. Fifty cents does not buy much of a meal. According to *Newsweek,* "For the first time since the Great Depression, homeless children are begging on the streets."[3]

Yet while the costs of food and other essentials have risen, and while the number of people needing help to survive has increased, the government has continued to cut programs and aid for the poor. Today, for example, fewer children receive a free school lunch than in 1980.[4]

For the families who come upon hard times, for the families unable to remain in their homes, for the families who take to the streets to survive, aid does not exist. It is only when a parent resorts to the welfare system, that they begin to receive help.

Homeless families who live in shelters and who sign up on all the proper lists and who have the knowledge and persistence to follow through with all the necessary paperwork, are eligible for a combination of benefits. But they must trek each day to the proper offices and have the strength to wait in all the lines that form each day at various welfare offices. The benefits they receive come from a number of sources. Twice-a-month payments from Aid to Families with Dependent Children are designed to meet basic costs of life. The amount varies with the number of children in the family. Food stamps pay for some food costs, and in some cities such as New York, an additional "restaurant allowance" of seventy-one cents per meal is intended to cover the higher costs of food when a family has no place to prepare its own meals and must eat in a restaurant. Families may also receive small amounts of money for transportation to search for housing, Medicaid for limited medical care, and WIC (Women, Infants, and Children) allotments for nutritional supplements for pregnant women and children under five.[5]

More often than not, people who should receive aid don't get it. According to Jonathan Kozol, for example, "more than half the women and children eligible for WIC in New York City don't receive it." Yet WIC was designed to prevent infant death or illness for all poor people.[6] Even when families go through the entire process and have proved themselves eligible for benefits, a process called "churning" in New York City may, without rhyme or reason, suddenly remove them from all the welfare lists and leave them without any benefits. According to the Community Service Society of New York, "churning" is designed to keep the welfare rolls current and to delete names of those families who no longer need aid from the welfare lists. Without regard for the eligibility of a family, welfare notifies the family that its benefits have been cut. The family must then reapply and once again prove that it is eligible. While this may seem an efficient means to keep welfare costs down, the family that has been cut sometimes is forced to survive for days with no money or food.

"Churning" is not the only cruelty built into the welfare system. Sometimes whole families are destroyed by this system. If a homeless husband and wife apply for AFDC, their social worker may decide that their children are endangered because they have no home. If that happens, the children can be taken away and placed in foster care. In addition to the emotional stress of having their children taken away, without them the parents are no longer eligible for AFDC benefits. Case closed. While it costs the state far more to care for a child under the foster care system, according to one lawyer in Los Angeles, this process occurs daily all over the United States. A couple waiting in a soup line in Oregon told Jonathan Kozol, "We had good work until last year. Since then we've had no home. Our kids were put in foster care."[7] At the time, the couple was sleeping on a plank under the Burnside Bridge, the sound of the traffic two feet above their heads.

If a husband is included on a woman's welfare budget—that is, if he is not working—and she must apply for shelter, he may or may not be allowed to live with his family. If he is allowed to live with the family and then finds some form of work, the family will have to forfeit all benefits. If he is caught hiding the fact that he works, the case will be closed and the family removed from the welfare rolls. Often a man who might be able to find at least temporary work, or work that pays far less than what it would cost to support his family, does not take the job, for fear of what it might mean for the welfare of his family.

If a husband is not included on a woman's welfare budget and she and the children are placed in a welfare hotel, he often must sign in to visit. Certain welfare hotels charge a fee for each visitor, so that not only has the family been separated, but the system even makes it difficult and expensive for a homeless father to visit his children.[8]

For kids without homes, the hardships involved in staying alive are different, depending primarily on their ages. But whether they are infants, toddlers, elementary-school-age children, preteens, teens, or young adults, the realities of homelessness make their lives both grim and dangerous.

STAYING ALIVE FOR INFANTS

The consequences of poverty begin before a homeless child is ever born. The care a mother is able to give herself while she is pregnant is the key factor influencing the health of the child she carries. Yet one out of every four pregnant women in the United States receives little or no prenatal care.[9] The United States, for all its wealth, for all the great strides it has made in medicine, and for all the high-tech facilities it has developed for medical care, remains far down on the infant-mortality list. It trails eighteen other nations in nurturing unborn children and preventing infant death.[10] According to Marilyn Gardner in the *Christian Science Monitor*.

> . . . *America represents a land of stark contrast for babies. At one extreme are the babies of affluence—newborn "princes" and "princesses." Planned for and wanted, they are monitored in the womb by sophisticated medical technology, then pampered after birth with $800 imported cribs, $300 strollers, infant gyms, and designer baby clothes.*[11]

At the other extreme are the babies of the poorest poor and the homeless. Gardner calls them a new "bio-underclass, disadvantaged almost from the moment of conception."[12] They are the product of poverty and its consequences. Drug and alcohol addiction and sexually transmitted diseases occur frequently among impoverished or homeless pregnant teens and adult women. The incidence of maternal anemia in pregnant women is also growing. Yet homeless mothers-to-be receive little or no prenatal care because they do not have the ability to pay for a doctor or because they cannot overcome the obstacles a poor mother must face to get free help. "I had to take four buses just to get to the clinic," an eighteen-year-old mother living at Covenant House told Gardner. "If the buses were late and I missed my appointment, I had to come back another day."[13]

According to the National Association of Children's Hospitals and the U.S. Department of Health and Human Services, infant-mortality rates have wors-

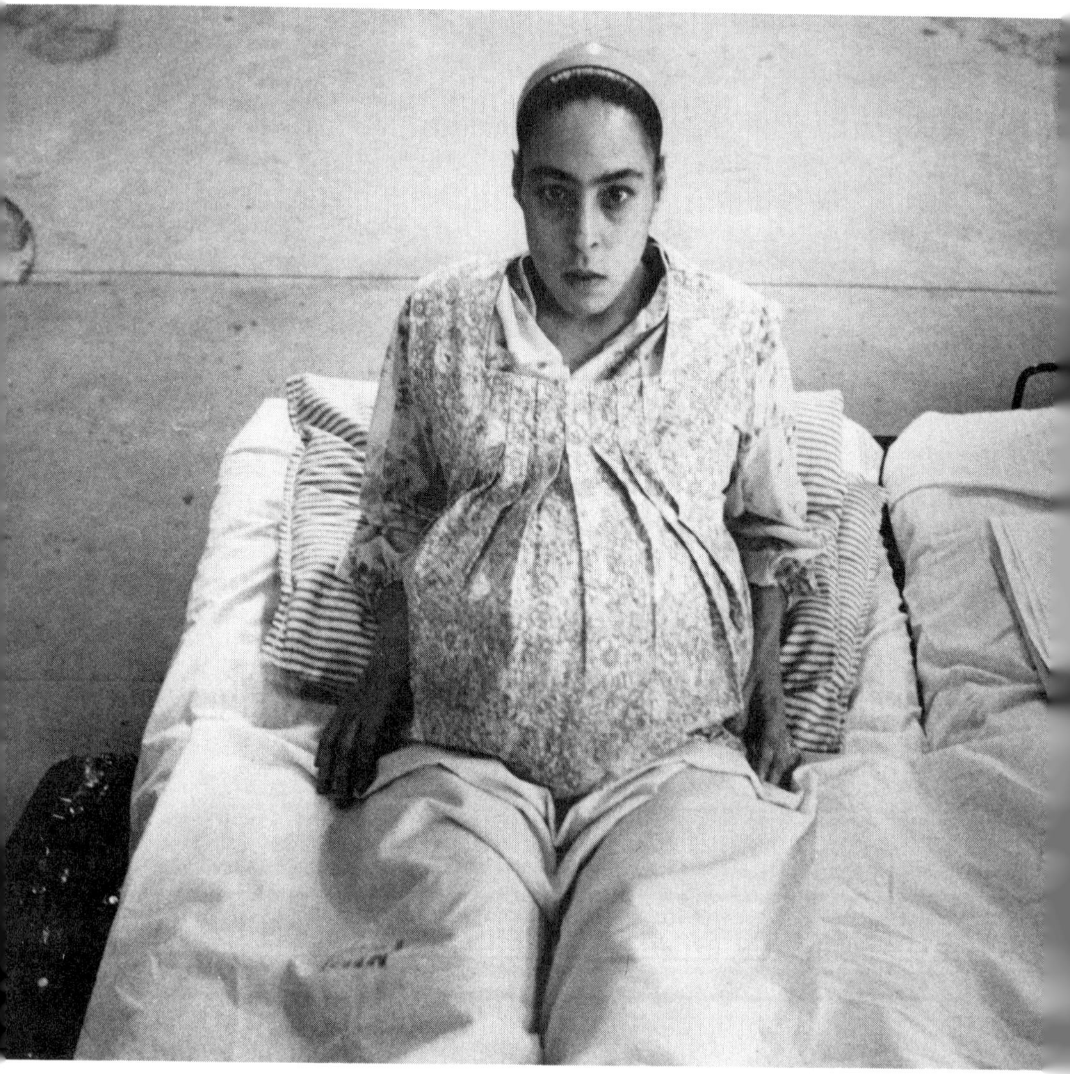

The terrible results of poverty and homelessness affect children even before they are born. This pregnant woman in a public shelter will not find it easy being a homeless mother—nor will the future appear better for her child.

ened for poor children, especially poor minority children. Nearly 40 percent of all black mothers receive no prenatal care in the first three months of their pregnancy. Black children are almost twice as likely to die in infancy as whites. In public housing projects, more than sixteen infants of every thousand die, regardless of color, and at a welfare hotel like the Martinique in New York City, that number is more like twenty-five out of every thousand.[14] Homelessness then may well determine whether a child will survive birth or its first few years.

Those children who die merely disappear. They will have no marker, no grave site, no memorial service, for their parents cannot afford these things. In New York City, infants are carted off with other poor and homeless corpses to Potter's Field, a public burial ground on an island off the city coast. It is also the site of a prison. The burials are performed by prisoners who stack coffins in trenches. Someday these areas will be bulldozed to make room for more coffins. Because the island is restricted, no one can attend the infants' funerals.

Those infants who somehow survive are not much better off. They are nine times more likely to be neurologically impaired, suffering from nervous system problems or brain disorders like fetal alcohol syndrome that will probably affect their ability to learn or their intelligence. Even if they survive, they are less likely to be able to cope with society or learn the skills they will need to become self-sufficient.

Many infants will never go home. Children who are born to homeless parents, who are born ill or drug addicted, or who are the children of teenage mothers who give them up to foster care, are sometimes kept in the hospital for months, even years. These children are called "boarder babies." Some have been kept so long that they are already walking. To protect them from harm because they cannot be constantly watched, they are tethered to their cribs. While nurses and volunteers try to make the lives of these children more bearable, they are not substitutes for a real family. "Infants held in hospitals so long," Jonathan Kozol warns, "are likely to grow retarded. Some, even after many months, have not been given names. Like their homeless parents in the city's shelters, they remain bed numbers."[15]

Finding homes for these boarder babies is a serious problem. Some will not be allowed to go to their parents for their own protection. These are usually the children of drug addicts. Others, who have been deserted (usually by teenage mothers), face a long wait before a foster parent can be found. For those with special problems, there is little hope of ever finding a home. In the *Christian Science Monitor,* Marilyn Gardner told of one thirteen-day-old baby, born three months prematurely to a cocaine-addicted mother. "Doctors say he is probably blind and suffers from seizures, among other grave complications. He will spend between six and nine months in this ward." Asked about his future, the doctor replied, "Nobody wants him."[16] Nor are there many foster homes available to babies who have contracted AIDS from their mothers. Few foster parents are willing to deal with the many problems of AIDS infants—the constant illnesses, the fears and prejudices surrounding the disease, and the fact that in the long run, these children will die.

STAYING ALIVE FOR CHILDREN

Those infants that do go home face an uncertain future.

In "Poverty's Legacy—Fragile Families, Vulnerable Babies," Marilyn Gardner describes the waiting room at Boston City Hospital in Massachusetts. Twice a week, the room is filled with malnourished children. The state funds this "failure to thrive" clinic, a term that has grown more and more common in the past ten years. Failure to thrive means that the child's life is in danger either because of its low birth weight or because after birth the child failed to gain weight normally. Seven of every ten children in the waiting room were born within the normal birth weight range. Yet in the time since birth, they have become malnourished. "In most cases people have a fairly intelligent notion of how to feed a child, but they can't afford to do it," Deborah Frank, director of the program, told Gardner. To keep the child satisfied and still its hungry cries, some mothers dilute the child's formula with water or feed the baby nondairy creamer. If they eat at all, older children often must survive on the cheapest foods, foods that do not meet the daily nutritional requirements for good health. For many families, the choice comes down to a "heat or eat" decision, especially in the cold winter months.[17] For others, the money is needed to find a job. One mother told another journalist:

> *At night I'd hear kids in the next tent crying because they hadn't eaten all day—or I'd hear their parents arguing over whether to spend their last two dollars on food or on gas to drive to a job-site the following day.*[18]

Parents are hard put to find money to buy food. In San Antonio, Texas, a father with two boys told Jonathan Kozol that while his family had been sleeping for four months next to a highway, he'd supported them by selling blood plasma to the "stab labs," places that pay for blood.[19] In cities, mothers are sometimes driven to sell their bodies as prostitutes to raise money to feed their kids.[20]

Yet while thousands of children fail to thrive each year, the government maintains policies that seem to ignore the plight of these desperate families. For example, it continues to pay over $1 million per day to store 2 billion pounds of surplus food in limestone caves in Kansas. While he was in office, former President Reagan delayed the $28 million that Congress allotted for the transportation of surplus food to poor people, nationwide.[21] "It's as though we don't exist," a father surviving on food given him by the Western Dairyland Economic Opportunity Council told John McCormick of *Newsweek.*[22] According to Marian Wright Edelman of the Children's Defense Fund, even when money could be made available by cutting luxury government spending, it is not done. Eliminating a single private dining room from the Pentagon's budget, she says, could restore to one million children who need it the morning snack program that was cut by the administration.[23]

Even when people are able to buy food, many homeless parents have no way to cook it without risking eviction from their temporary shelter. At many of the welfare hotels, no stove or refrigerator is provided. Many families have to use the bathtub as a kitchen sink. Cooking, if it is done at all, is managed on illegal hot plates, and served to children who sit on the floor or on their beds. Without a hot plate, families are forced to live on a diet of canned goods, dry cereals, and other nonperishable items. Because they have no refrigerator, formula for infants must be stored on the windowsill in cold weather and in toilet tanks during the warmer months.

The lack of proper nutrition coupled with the circumstances of homelessness have had a profound effect on the health of children without homes. Many of

In many cases, the street is the only place for homeless children to play.

the shelters available to families, especially the welfare hotels, are dirty and parasite-infested. Families are forced to live in crowded rooms, placing their babies in boxes or drawers because their requests for cribs go unheeded. Some of the rooms are so small that when the children's cots are open, the bathroom door cannot be opened. The stress created by the living conditions in emergency welfare housing is often so great, especially for single mothers, that they abandon their children to the foster care system.

Stress also affects the health of children. They must be closely controlled while living in either barracks shelters or hotels. They are unable to play freely, to run, to jump, or to shout as children with homes can. Most barracks shelters have rules that are very strict. Children must remain with their parents in the small cubicles allotted them so that other families may also have privacy. In barracks shelters, there is little room to play, and parents are required to keep the children quiet. Even when they are placed in hotels or semi-permanent welfare housing, children must be constrained. Because welfare hotels are often located in crime-ridden areas of cities, parents do not dare let their children play outside. Even the corridors of these hotels can be dangerous.

According to the study *Homelessness, Health, and Human Needs,* completed by the Institute of Medicine, homeless children suffer from more frequent recurrences of physical disorders and from illnesses that last far longer than those experienced by the rest of the nation's children. In addition to malnutrition, many children suffer from anemia, a condition in which the blood lacks the necessary amount of red blood cells or the necessary level of hemoglobin. Anemic children appear pallid and weak. Often their heartbeats are irregular. Asthma, an allergic condition that leads to difficulty in breathing and other respiratory disorders, is another common ailment of homeless children. Half of all homeless children either receive no immunizations for such dangerous illnesses as diphtheria, tetanus, measles, and polio, or they receive them late, putting them at high risk for contracting a serious illness that could have been prevented. Overall, the rate of chronic disorders for homeless kids is almost twice that of children nationally.[24]

Another disturbing trend has been the increase in lead poisoning noted recently by health officials in New York City. Lead poisoning is caused by eating the paint chips that flake off the crumbling walls of older buildings. Small children, curious and sometimes hungry, are prone to tasting these chips. Because of that, lead-based paint was banned many years ago. In the tenements and welfare hotels, in the condemned buildings and shacks in which homeless people take shelter, however, lead paint has not been covered or removed. Because lead can accumulate in the body, it can cause swelling of the brain tissue and damage the nerves there and elsewhere in the body. It can also cause permanent, and sometimes fatal, kidney injury.

Not only do homeless children suffer more from illness, but curing their illnesses is much more difficult. The government has cut the amount of money it has been spending on health-care clinics for welfare families. Many health-care facilities that were formerly funded by the government have since had to close. Getting sick children to a doctor is difficult for homeless parents, especially when they have little money for transportation.

Because homeless children rarely have a family pediatrician and often move from one area to another, health records become an additional problem. Doctors often have to make a diagnosis without the aid of a health history, which can help pinpoint medical problems or patterns.

Even when doctors know the problem, homeless families may have difficulty following the doctor's orders. Many eat in soup kitchens and sleep in a different place each night. They carry all their worldly goods with them. Medicines may be lost, or the child may not be able to take the prescribed medication at the proper times. Getting the bed rest necessary to become well again can be impossible when a family is living out of a car or being shuffled from one shelter to another. And if the illness requires the refrigerated storage of medicine or a special diet, as with diabetes, a family may find it impossible to follow the medical advice of a clinic doctor. According to "The Unhealthy Homeless" in *The Futurist,* "even if the health care services that are needed . . . were widely available and accessible, the impact of such services would be severely restricted as long as patients remained on the streets or in emergency shelters."[25]

The psychological scars of being homeless compound the health problems of youngsters without homes. Studies cited by the Institute of Medicine show that homeless children "suffer greater emotional and developmental problems."[26] Dr. Ellen Bassuk, a psychiatrist participating in a Harvard Medical School study of eighty-two homeless families, found that many of her patients were experiencing strange and ominous problems. In families that had moved at least five times, one nine-year-old talked about wanting to die. Another yanked out three of his teeth. He was worried, he told Dr. Bassuk. Other toddlers mentioned in the study had reverted to crawling. Many were awakened by frightening nightmares; others reverted to bed-wetting, began sleepwalking, or developed violent mood swings and severe depression.[27]

In "Children of the Homeless," *U.S. News & World Report* described children in a Portland, Oregon, shelter who blamed themselves for their parents' despair. Many felt so ashamed that they could not look at themselves in a mirror.[28] Such shame is not restricted just to the children of the homeless. Parents feel it too. "You can always tell the family. . . . that's new to the shelter," observed one Wisconsin priest in Kozol's *Rachel and Her Children.* "Their heads are always down . . . they're very grateful for everything. They eat very quickly, and then they disappear."[29] The shame, says Kozol, is worsened by the constant need to line up, by having a number, and by being allowed only one serving. "People who, one month before, may have been strong and full of pride are humbled rapidly," he states.

No matter how careful and compassionate shelter workers might be in calling their clients "guests," being made to feel inferior, being shamed, inevitably leads to anger. For children, unable to understand their situation or to verbalize their fears, that anger is either turned inward upon themselves or it explodes outwardly, in hostile behavior in the shelters, in schools, or on the streets. When their situation continues, children lose hope. Many talk of being unable to breathe; others of wanting to die.

Harvard psychiatrist Alvin Poussaint believes that those early feelings of failure, self-doubt, and hostility will accompany poor and homeless children throughout their childhood. "For every talent poverty has stimulated, it has blighted a hundred,"[30] former HEW Secretary John Gardner stated. The consequence is a generation of children whose problems will follow them, and, as a result, whose lives will continue to affect the nation as a whole.

STAYING ALIVE FOR ADOLESCENTS

For kids growing up homeless and for adolescent kids becoming homeless for the first time, prospects grow even dimmer. Whether they have been exposed to it throughout their childhood or whether they are experiencing it for the first time, the view from poverty's side is traumatic. Children living in welfare hotels, shelters, or on the streets observe a daily sideshow of the worst of human behavior. They see crime, from petty theft to gang fights to grisly murders. They see prostitution, both women and men offering the use of their bodies for money. They see drug addiction everywhere, if not in their own parents or brothers and sisters, certainly everywhere around them in shelters and on the streets. They see staggering drunks and mentally ill adults dazedly picking through the garbage or ranting their way up and down the street. In their schools (if they attend), on the streets, and even in the hotels and projects in which they live, homeless kids must learn the age-old dictum of do unto others before they do unto you, because the circumstances in which they live demand it. In the world of poverty, the only way to escape being a victim is to become a predator.

The consequence of homelessness is that teenagers with physical and emotional problems, without an education, without job skills, and for the most part, without much self-esteem or hope, are more likely to ensnare themselves in the very traps that lead to even greater desperation. Girls tend to become pregnant quite early, some as young as twelve or thirteen. Nearly half a million children are born to teenage mothers each year, most of them without a home.[31] Their children will be less likely to have a father. They, like many of their mothers, will become the new generation of welfare mothers, babies raising babies. Of one 4-pound baby being dressed to go home to his fifteen-year-old mother and her ten-month-old first child, a nurse at one Florida hospital said: "He's going to be another toy for her to play with. It's pointless to try to teach her about parenting. She's not going to do it when she gets home."

Many teenagers, yearning for stability, love, and security, will fall prey to pimps, who will lead them into a life of prostitution. In "Coming of Age on the City Streets," Patricia Hersch quotes Katie, a former prostitute and street kid since she was twelve:

> *Anywhere out here, there are ways to make money. Legitimate work? No. There's no doors open to us . . . How are you going to be able to hold down a job if you have no high school diploma, if you're not able to take a shower every day, if you don't have clean clothes to wear to work?*[32]

They are deficient, these young people who have not had the opportunity to work through the normal growth stages necessary to becoming a healthy adult. Trudee Able-Peterson, director of the Streetwork Project, an outreach program in New York City, told Hersch of another girl she had worked with. Her name was Amy and she had been a prostitute since she was twelve. What did she want for her eighteenth birthday, the director asked her. Her reply was that she wanted a coloring book and crayons.[33]

Because they are caught in a world of drugs and prostitution, homeless teens stand a far greater chance of contracting venereal diseases such as syphilis, and today, of dying from the deadly AIDS virus. The AIDS virus infects them either from sexual relations with infected partners, many of them drug abusers, or from using dirty needles themselves. Jim Kennedy, a physician and medical director of Covenant House, told *Psychology Today:* "Even if these girls never end up working as prostitutes, they are at risk when they have sex with the drug-abusing guys who control the street life of local neighborhoods."[34] Of four girls Kennedy tested who fit this profile, three tested positive for AIDS. One of the three was pregnant. Kennedy believes that of the 11,000 kids who have been in and out of Covenant House in any one year, probably 15 percent would test AIDS positive. Of those who are prostituting every night, he guesses probably half have the disease.[35] While *The New England Journal of Medicine* reports that a study analyzing military applicants shows "a very small number" of AIDS infection in adolescents nationwide, rates from the large cities are ten in every thousand. That rate doubles to twenty in every thousand in cities such as New York, San Francisco, and Washington, D.C., the cities to which homeless kids gravitate. Because the latency period between infection and the appearance of AIDS symptoms may be over ten years, however, many experts believe these adolescents will become part of a third wave of the AIDS epidemic that will only begin to show itself in the next decade.[36]

Despite the number of organizations that are attempting to educate young street people about the dangers of drug use and prostitution, most of the people Patricia Hersch interviewed did not believe they were making any progress in changing street kids' behavior:

> *The teens won't remember; they will reason it is OK to have sex with friends; some girls want to get pregnant; their johns give them more money if they don't use a condom. Mostly, though, there are so many ways to die every day on the street that they cannot focus on something that may kill them years from now.*[37]

For teenagers on the streets, drugs and alcohol can lead to even greater disintegration of their lives.

Another teen told *Newsweek:* "I know all that [they're teaching] makes sense. But the thing is, when you want drugs bad enough, seconds count."[38]

When they do discover they have AIDS, many street kids have no option but to continue life as they have known it—even if that means infecting others with their disease. Many have ceased to care about life altogether:

> *You know, I once took four hits of acid, double-soaked. That's like taking eight hits at once. Then I walked across a high bridge, figuring I wouldn't make it and that would be fine. I would look at AIDS the same way. That's what street life is like. You learn to survive. But you also learn not to care if you don't.*[39]

If a young person survives the crime, drugs, and diseases of the street, the effect of street life takes its toll in other ways. A study done in 1983 by the New York State Psychiatric Institute found that "shelter users have a psychiatric profile . . . similar to that of . . . adolescents attending a psychiatric clinic. A third were depressed and 18 percent antisocial. One-fourth of them had considered suicide and an additional fourth had actually attempted it."[40] Another study by the National Network places that figure much higher; it found that 66 percent either consider or attempt suicide.[41]

According to a study done by Friedland and Marotto cited in *The Futurist,* "Homelessness itself may create mental problems for a large number of the homeless in the future. . . . Those not joining the ranks of the homeless from mental institutions may soon find that being on the street makes them crazy."[42]

Hospitals are not equipped to deal with the growing mental crises that young street people are experiencing. Most emergency shelters allow a stay of only fifteen days, not nearly enough time for a psychiatrist to help or for a young person to get well. Mental health facilities are also filled to the brim with mentally ill adults, who, according to most experts, comprise over a third of all homeless people. Many of these adults would have been kept in institutions a few decades ago, but in 1963, the federal government passed a law that required the release of all mental patients who were not a danger to themselves or society. With the passing of that law and the subsequent release of thousands of people ill-equipped to care for themselves, the government promised to fund local mental health clinics to help released mental patients adjust to society and become self-sufficient. Unfortunately, these community treatment centers never materialized. Even when clinics are available, mentally ill patients are the least likely to recognize that they need help or to go to such clinics, and because of the civil liberties laws, no mentally ill person can be forced into treatment against his will. While many states have developed "outreach" programs to help mentally ill adults find housing and therapy, in no state has enough money been allotted to change the situation.

Unfortunately, the "deinstitutionalization" of mental patients and the trend toward admitting fewer people to state mental hospitals; general hospitals; rehabilitation, correctional, and mental retardation facilities has had dire results. Many of these people have become heads of families, the fathers and mothers of children they are not emotionally equipped to raise. This has made life even more difficult for kids without homes.

Yet even in families headed by the strongest, most mentally-balanced parents, homelessness is undermining the promise and destroying the chances of vast numbers of children without homes. While more and more fathers and mothers fall below the poverty line, unable to provide even the most basic shelter, food, clothing, and medical care for their children, more and more children will be subjected to the degradation of living in cars, tents, barracks shelters, and welfare hotels. The physical and mental health of these children cannot improve. Nor can they maintain the hope for a better life when so many doors are closed to them. As we shall see in the next chapter, homelessness is destroying even the best chance kids without homes may have to climb out of poverty: the chance for an education.

CHAPTER 4
GETTING AN EDUCATION

It is safe to say that most low-income people stay poor because they cannot get better-paying jobs. Ill health or physical disability prevents some people from working. Generally, however, poor people cannot meet the requirements for better-paying jobs. Sadly, many are intellectually capable, but because they have never gotten the academic or vocational education they need to compete in the workplace, they are disqualified by employers who would otherwise hire them.

For poor children then, education is a necessity. Whether poor children will live the rest of their lives poor, or raise themselves out of poverty will depend almost entirely on whether they can prepare themselves for the jobs of the future. They can accomplish that only by going to school regularly and by being willing and able to learn.

Job qualifications are different today than they have been in the past. The United States was once an agricultural nation, a country whose major occupation and source of income was the production of food. Sometime during the 1800s, that changed. With the industrial revolution—the coming of machines, and assembly lines that could mass-produce everything from shoes to typewriters—the primary workplace of United States citizens shifted from rural farms to urban factories. It was not difficult for an unskilled farm laborer with only a rudimentary education to learn how to run a factory machine. Because the assembly line allowed the production of a product to be broken down into easily learnable parts, a farmhand who moved to the city could find work, whether he had advanced reading, writing, and mathematical skills or not. In comparison to the demands placed on workers today, the transition from an agricultural to an industrial economy was easy.

Today, the economy of the United States is once again in transition. Slowly at first, and then with increasing speed, in the last few decades the nature of work in the United States has been shifting. Few new jobs today require manual skills, and those assembly-line jobs that have traditionally been open to workers have decreased. The mass production of the things United States citizens always made for themselves is now frequently done in other countries, where labor is cheaper. In addition, many simple and even some complex operations required to produce a product are now performed by machines controlled by computers. Both trends have reduced the need for unskilled and semiskilled workers. Instead, highly trained workers, who can understand and utilize computers, who can work more easily with their minds than with their hands, are now needed. Unfortunately, those educationally unprepared for or incapable of such work can find only very low-paying jobs. While nothing is wrong with doing unskilled work, these jobs do not pay enough to support a family.

While once only a rudimentary knowledge of reading and math was necessary to survive, now young people must be educated if they are to be eligible for tomorrow's jobs. Young people growing up will need at least a high school diploma, if not a college degree, to be able to compete for jobs that will support them and their families. Failure to get that education will place obstacles in the paths of even the brightest students who drop out of school. Those obstacles may well prevent their ever breaking the cycle of poverty.

Meanwhile, the number of people who cannot read or write has continued to increase to an estimated 30 million Americans, and the gap between the wealthiest and the poorest Americans grows wider. Today, the richest twenty out of every hundred Americans earn 44 percent, almost half of the national family income, while the poorest twenty earn only 4.6 percent of the national family income.[1] This means that the richest people will have plenty of money to buy homes and cars, driving prices up, while the poorest people will have to survive on one-eighth as much money.

To be able to increase their share of the wealth, kids without homes and those in families living below the poverty level need an education more than anyone. Unfortunately, they are the least likely to get it. With the exception of the children of migrant workers, homeless kids will find it hardest of all to get an education because they are the least likely to remain in one school district long enough to complete thirteen years of continuous schooling. Every break in that continuity makes it harder for students to keep up. Consequently, their chances of dropping behind and finally dropping out of school are increased. In some homeless families, parents are often forced to move many times in search of work. In others, parents are unemployed, living in temporary shelters that may be changed at any time. Kids who cannot live with their parents may be placed by the state in foster homes far from where they were born. And for kids living on the streets, getting an education is nearly an impossibility.

GETTING ENROLLED

Every time a homeless family moves, the children must be enrolled in a new school. Until recently, some communities set up roadblocks that made it difficult, if not impossible, to meet the enrollment requirements. They required parents to produce proof of residency in the community, birth certificates, immunization and health records, and their child's past school records. Gathering such information, if it could be gathered at all, took days, weeks, and sometimes even months for parents already beset with the problems of finding work or food to eat. Families living in shelters or campgrounds or temporarily doubled up could not meet the communities' residency requirements. Kids without homes were therefore forbidden to enroll in school.

Finally, the federal government realized that something had to be done to reinforce the fact that all children have a right to an education. In 1987, in order to insure that the fifty states protected that right, Congress passed the Stewart B. McKinney Homeless Assistance Act (P.L. 100–77). Among other forms of help to the homeless, the McKinney Act required all states to ensure homeless children an education and granted funds to develop programs to help them do so.[2] Homeless kids were exempted by law from the local residency requirements that many communities had used to keep them out of school. Henceforward, children living in shelters could no longer be considered nonresidents.

Yet despite the laws that now protect the right to an education, many communities continue to balk at enrolling students they do not consider their responsibility. *Newsweek* cited the case of the Montgomery family, who in 1989 moved from Arizona to the Wompatuck State Park in Massachusetts. Since the area of the park in which they camped was part of the town of Hingham, the Montgomerys tried to register their children in the Hingham public schools. The school committee refused them enrollment, claiming that camping in a state park did not give them the right to attend school in the district in which the park was located. Finally, after much publicity, the neighboring town of Norwell agreed to take the children.[3]

When families are involuntarily moved to shelters distant from the place where they live, they are also forced to move far from their schools. Much of what makes school a safe and pleasurable experience depends on the permanence of school, of being familiar with the building, the teachers, and the other students. Children are far more secure and far more likely to succeed when they know what is expected of them. Being shifted from one school to another adds to the already painful stress of being homeless. According to the *New York Times,* for example, more children live in temporary emergency housing in New York than in any other state. Of possibly as many as 25,000 homeless children, nearly 5,000 have been sheltered outside of the city, disrupting their schooling, even if the schools in the town to which they've moved welcomed them. The problem is the same in many other states as well.

Hoping to make things a little easier, in 1981, Boston adopted a "controlled choice" plan that allowed students, including those who are homeless, to attend the school of their choice anywhere in the Boston school district. Following the Boston example, New York's Education Department passed new regulations in 1989 that allowed parents to choose the school to

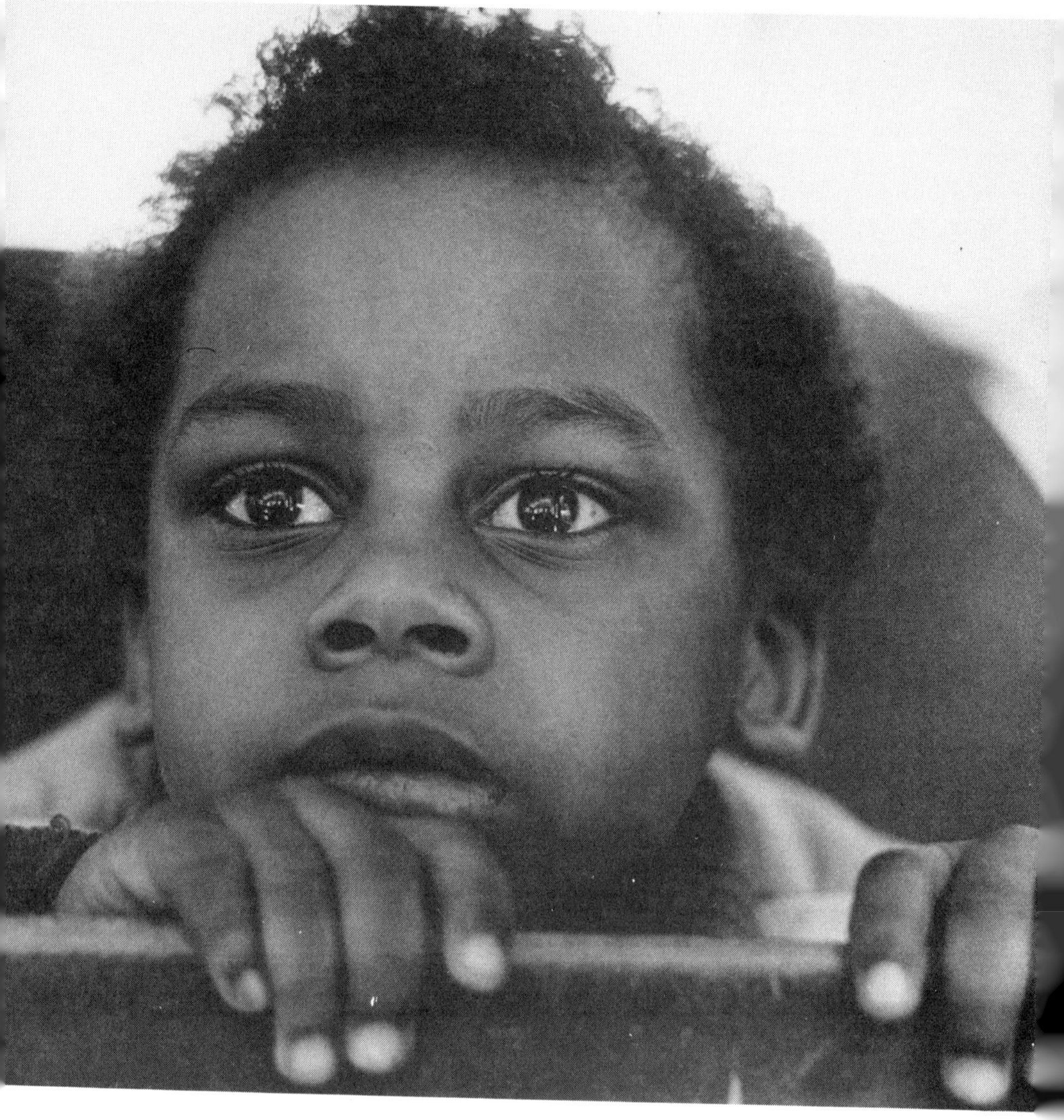

This child from a welfare hotel is picked up and transported each day to a school many miles away—another hardship that homeless children often must bear.

which they send their children. Now parents sheltered far from the city can require the county social service department in their district to provide transportation each day back to their child's former school.

This has also helped to solve another potential problem the schools faced. Many of the towns in which New York City set up emergency overflow shelters were not prepared to deal with a sudden increase in students, especially an increase of students with the many learning problems homeless kids often have. Town administrators feared that their schools would be overwhelmed with scores of children needing special help. Although the state assured towns that it would reimburse them for additional classrooms, teachers, and materials, most towns found that their worries were groundless. Few experienced large increases in students needing special education, and over half of New York's shelter parents chose to keep their children in their original schools.

Although allowing parents to choose their children's school has eliminated some of the problems getting children enrolled can create, in some ways the solution has created additional problems. In Westchester County, New York, for example, the shortage of low-cost welfare housing has meant that over 454 children have to be housed in other counties. That means that students have to travel as much as ninety minutes by taxi or mini-van to their former schools. According to one official quoted in *Rachel and Her Children,* "Many of these children rise so early that they don't eat breakfast and arrive at school carsick and hungry. . . . We have children as young as four years old traveling over thirty miles . . ."[4]

ATTENDING SCHOOL

While easing restrictions and requirements for enrollment has been a step in the right direction, the next step, getting children to come to school regularly, continues to be a serious obstacle. Many families who move often can't see any point in going through the enrollment process when they may be on the road again in a few days. The Orange County, California *Register* described how each day while they should have been in school, Cynthia Stowers and her brother, John Riddle, killed time in the park playing tag, watching the squirrels, or flying a kite. Their mother told the *Register,* "It's too hard to keep the kids in school when we move every few days between shelters and parks."[5] Cynthia and John had played hooky nearly the last two months of school.

According to the National Coalition for the Homeless, possibly as many as three-quarters of a million American children are homeless. Well over half of those children do not attend school regularly. Another study done by the U.S. Conference of Mayors found that 43 percent do not attend school at all.[6] Even though the law requires all children between the ages of five and sixteen to attend school, school officials cannot enforce it. A family living in a campground may move without notice; a shelter family is frequently transferred. One day a child is in school, the next, he or she may be gone. Schools do not have the staff to track so many homeless children, even in rural areas. In the cities, the task of keeping track of the millions of school-age children is impossible.

School officials have found that easing enrollment requirements does not solve the problem. Just opening the doors to homeless children is not enough. "They don't come out on their own as much as we'd like," one school official told the *New York Times.* "There is a shyness. We have to go to them. And there has to be a bus service to bring the children to school."[7]

Despite the difficulty in tracking children, some school administrators try. In District 10 of the Bronx in New York City, an attendance officer and family worker go each morning to the Thorpe Family Residence—where Jessica and Christopher fled their rat-infested apartment—to try to convince parents to get their children to school. Many times, parents resist. "A lot of mothers went through trauma in the hotels, so the tendency is always to stay together and travel together," Luisa Pineiro Fuentes told the *New York Times.* "The families come in disoriented. They don't know the neighborhood. They don't know where the bodega [grocery store] is. They don't know who the principal is."[8] Many times they claim that the children have appointments at clinics or that they need their children with them at the welfare office.

Many of these parents are "decent, down-to-earth folks who truly care and want more for their children than a single 10-foot-by-12-foot room,"[9] Terrence Quinn, another school official, told the *Times.* But homelessness changes priorities and makes people anxious. The unfortunate effect is that children who are bounced from one place to another, from one school to another, lose both the desire and habit of going to school. The typical homeless high school student attends school only half of the time. "They are urban nomads. . . . They are our most abused children,"[10] another New York principal said.

FEELINGS ABOUT SCHOOL

When Jessica's mother moved her family to the Thorpe shelter, Jessica began going to school in District 10 of New York City. Her grades improved. Part of her success was due to the new safety her family felt in the shelter, and part to the efforts her school made to help her. Jessica even won a trip to the Big Apple Circus for her perfect attendance, a strong indicator of how she feels about school. Cynthia Stowers, who had to kill time in a park in California, also loved school, but homelessness had forced her to miss so many months that she had gone from winning spelling and speech contests to flunking ninth grade. She told the Orange County, California *Register*, "I miss having something to go to in the daytime. Sometimes you wish you could go to school so you can get away from your family for a while. School is fun to me . . . an education is the most important thing in the world."[11]

But Cynthia's brother tells another story, a story much more typical of how homeless kids feel about going to school. Kids picked on him; they didn't like his shirt, his pants, or his haircut. "That's why I hate school," John said. "If there wasn't all those kids, I'd love school."[12]

While schoolchildren can be notoriously cruel to each other, homeless kids are even more frequently the targets of prejudice and the butt of jeering and derision by other children. Christine Klatt, who moved with her family from Ontario, said that there is a special kind of shame in being homeless. She tried to keep it a secret. "I did tell one friend, but Vanessa, she told one boy and the boy looked at me and said, 'She's a dump.' "[13] Being different can be difficult even for adults, but at an age when young people will do anything to be like their friends, being tagged a "dump" or other, even crueler names, can be traumatic.

According to *Newsweek*, even teachers can be put off by the appearance of "the hotel children." Because often they are unable to bathe, they sometimes smell. Sometimes they look sickly, possibly even diseased. The other children don't want to sit next to them and their teachers stay distant, too.

Some young people still try to do their best to appear normal. Another homeless boy the *Register* interviewed explained: "At school I am talking and smiling all the time like it's no problem. You could go to any of my schools and ask any teacher, 'Does he get moody and does he withdraw from people?' And they'll say, 'No.' "[14] But even when they begin to make friends, kids without homes find it hard to build friendships because they can't plan after-school activities. Jennifer Klatt explained: "All my friends are like, 'Call me tonight' and I'm like, 'I can't,' and they're like, 'How can I contact you?' and I'm like, 'It's hard.' "[15]

Homeless kids also find it difficult to allow themselves to grow attached to school friends. They never know when they will move next. It's hard leaving people they've grown to like, so many learn to keep their distance. Then it's not so painful when their families have to pull up stakes.

PERFORMANCE IN SCHOOL

A study completed by Ellen Bassuk, associate professor of psychiatry at Harvard Medical School, found that homeless children's performance in school is poor. Four of every ten students she surveyed were failing or doing below-average work. Half had repeated at least one grade. One fourth of all homeless kids were in special education classes. While nationally, only sixteen of every hundred kids with permanent homes suffered from a serious developmental delay, that number increased to fifty-four of every hundred among homeless kids.[16]

"The cards are stacked against homeless children: they have no quiet place to study or to rest; they don't know where their next shelter will be; they are surrounded by drugs and often by violence," Terrence Quinn told the *New York Times.*[17] Despite these handicaps, one youngster he knew from a New York shelter had managed to become valedictorian of her class. She is an example of those children who somehow manage not to give up, but she is a rarity. More often than not, children who must face the daily hardships of homelessness falter.

Many fall hopelessly behind, making it increasingly difficult for them to remain motivated. One student told reporter Melissa Weiner how it felt to move from one school where he was doing well to another, where the classes had progressed much farther:

> *It feels horrible. You feel so stupid. "God," you just keep saying, "Why me?" This horrible pressure's just on you all the time, and you can't get rid of it. You wake up one morning, and you realize it's still there. You can't get rid of it."*[18]

Children can leave a school where their class is learning multiplication, only to find that in the next school, the same grade is already learning fractions. In one school, they may be writing simple paragraphs, while in the next the teacher assigns thesis-based essays. Often, they struggle to catch up only to move again. They might just become interested in the unit one class is studying on weather and have to leave. When they begin again in another school, no such unit is being taught. It is hard to feel any subject is important when the continuity of what they are being taught is so fractured. It is hard to stay motivated when their education is such a struggle to keep up. Diane Doherty, Georgetown University's program director for disadvantaged children, explained:

> *Think about what it's like to be ten years old and you don't know where you're going to sleep, but you do know that you have to go to school the next day and you must get started on a science project, too.*[19]

Because chunks of time are spent absent from school, homeless youngsters frequently must repeat grades, making them the oldest and sometimes the biggest in their classes. Homeless kids are twice as likely to repeat grades.[20] Each time they fail, their self-esteem lessens. And they do not have the support of friends. Other students, unaware of the difficulties these youngsters face, think they're stupid, adding to their already poor self-image.

When they are tested, homeless kids fare poorly on the standardized exams that schools use to decide a student's placement. Only 40 percent of New York's homeless schoolchildren place at or above grade level on the state's standardized reading test in comparison to three-quarters of all other students.[21] Yet even when their lack is pinpointed, they often do not get the special services available to other students, such as remedial reading, bilingual classes, and talented and gifted classes. Once again, homelessness deprives them of their right to an appropriate education.

Even from their earliest years, homeless children are deprived of the very programs that could make a difference in their school performance. Headstart and Title XX federal funds for day-care programs are designed to give children the opportunity and encourage a desire to learn when they are young. Yet these programs reach as few as 16 percent of the children that are eligible for Headstart and only 7 percent of those eligible for Title XX.[22]

Children Today describes some of the problems young homeless children display, often because they are denied the learning opportunities kids with permanent homes take for granted. Most have no formal group play experience. They do not have a neighborhood to play in or a home to which they can invite other children. They do not know how to get along well with other children, nor have they learned the sharing skills that can help them to make friends. They hoard toys and have trouble waiting their turn to play or to receive snacks. At mealtime, many gorge their food, hoping for extra helpings. They often lack self-control and respond impulsively to frustration or stress. They frequently interfere with others, intruding upon games or work. Keeping their attention on an activity or concentrating is difficult for them. Not only do they use classroom materials inappropriately—painting or marking walls, for example—but they treat their classmates more as objects, often seemingly unaware of their presence.

Their behavior is not surprising. New York's District 10 director of programs for homeless and relocated children describes their feelings:

> *Imagine you're in a house where your mother slowly built up her china and put up her curtains, and then the building burns down and you don't have anything except your pajamas. You go to someone's house and maybe you go to someone else's house and then you go to a congregate shelter and you sleep in a bunk bed with other families around you, maybe witnessing sexual activity. Then maybe you end up in a hotel in one room with no kitchen, sleeping altogether in one place . . .*[23]

When Renee Carter and her two children moved to a Salvation Army shelter in Baltimore, she watched helplessly as her eight-year-old son's grades dropped from average to failing. "He's sulky and fighting all the time," she told *U.S. News & World Report.*[24] Her complaint is typical. Many otherwise normal and healthy children soon begin to show signs of the stress being homeless creates. According to Jonathan Kozol, school officials see homeless children becoming "deeply troubled," often withdrawing or becoming hyperactive.[25] Some physically abuse themselves; others are mistrustful of their classmates and teachers, feeling isolated and frightened.

EDUCATIONAL OBSTACLES

Homelessness takes its toll on students by making it harder for them to seize the opportunities an education affords. Unfortunately, the schools they attend may add to their problems. While some school systems are actively trying everything within their means to get homeless kids to school and to help them achieve, many more do little or nothing in the form of "outreach" or enforcing the enrollment regulations properly. This is especially true in smaller cities and rural areas. "We're totally forgotten," Patricia Sher, executive director of one shelter in Syracuse told the *New York Times.*

Part of the problem has to do with the amount of money school districts have to spend per pupil. Schools are primarily supported by the taxes levied on residents of their area. Wealthy towns are able to have their pick of teachers and can support better programs because they have more money. Classes are usually smaller. Teachers are able to order the materials they need, are often supported in the classroom by an aide, and are afforded more free time to plan lessons. Unfortunately, most homeless kids do not go to such schools. Instead, they are likely to attend schools so underfunded that, like those in Chicago, they cannot even afford to hire substitutes. On an average morning in Chicago, 5,700 children, enough to fill 190 classrooms, come to school only to find they have no teacher. "We've been in this typing class a whole semester," one student told Jonathan Kozol, "and they still can't find us a teacher."[26] Most homeless kids go to schools that have "crumbling buildings, outdated texts and a shortage of basics such as paper and pens."[27]

In addition, children who are "poor, black, or Hispanic," as are many homeless kids, face a "subtle and destructive form of discrimination" in school. According to the National Coalition of Advocates for Students, they are far more likely to be disciplined—either physically, or through suspension or expulsion—than other students.[28] They are also more likely to be placed in vocational education classes or special classes for the "mildly mentally handicapped."[29]

"Tracking," that is, placing students in classes based on how they perform on standardized tests, has long been an accepted means of separating kids in order to meet their specific needs. Lately this practice has come under fire. Many parents and educators believe that "tracking" makes it extremely difficult for a student to get back into mainstream, or regular classes. As one parent told *U.S. News & World Report:*

> *That blue slip is really a one-way ticket to emotional and educational death for many children. It says to a child, "You are retarded." It says to a child, "You are lost."*[30]

Whether tracking makes it impossible for a child to catch up or not has yet to be proved. But homeless kids attending the poorest schools are often assigned to classes that contain large numbers, where maintaining discipline rather than fostering learning preoccupies the teacher. There is little dispute about how much a child can learn in classes that are too large for special attention, or in classes where students' misbehavior takes up most of the classes' time.

MEETING THE NEEDS OF HOMELESS CHILDREN

Everyone agrees that homeless children have special needs that must be met if they are to succeed in school. Yet many disagree on what the schools should do. One new practice that has come under a lot of fire is the "shelter school." Shelter schools have been set up in some districts such as Santa Clara and San Diego, California; Salt Lake City, Utah; and Tacoma, Washington, in rooms or buildings adjacent to the shelters in which students live. Shelter schools solve many problems. Enrolling a student in a public school when that student may be moved only a week later creates problems both for the child and the school. In so short a time, a teacher has little chance to get to know a child, let alone to offer help. A shelter teacher, working with smaller groups of students who all have similar problems, is more likely to be able to address those problems. As one administrator of the Tacoma public schools explained:

> *We try to take care of "belly needs" with solid meals before we take care of "mind needs." Homeless youngsters have significant needs, and if they are going to be successful in education, we need to treat their other problems.*[31]

At the Emergency Lodge in Chicago, Illinois, the Salvation Army Child Care Program began a separate program for homeless preschool children aged three to five in 1982. Two years later, administrators added a home visiting program to help children and their parents after they find homes. The Emergency Lodge is a temporary shelter that services families in crisis. Many

These bright-eyed children attend the Salvation Army's Emergency Lodge Playschool in Chicago. Here children are not scorned for being homeless, or punished for acting out. Their teachers know how to help them with their problems.

arrive at the shelter after a fire or an eviction, while others may be fleeing domestic violence. Many of the families the Lodge serves have a history of instability, and their children are at risk. A family's average stay at the Lodge is two to three weeks. While they are there, homeless preschoolers attend the Playschool. The Playschool's goals are specifically designed to help children in crisis—to foster emotional development and to reduce the stress they are experiencing. Teachers encourage these children to express their feelings and needs, especially their fears about being homeless. Free play is especially important, and table games and art, water, and sand play take up much of the time. Conflict, testing, and acting out, behavior frowned upon in most preschool programs, are expected and accepted at the Playschool. Teachers use these situations to help their pupils learn social skills, express their ideas, and learn to negotiate.

Since all of their classmates are homeless, too, students do not have to face the prejudice—the name-calling or the shame of being different—that often occurs in a regular classroom. Advocates of shelter schools claim that this allows students a chance to build some self-confidence.

On the other hand, critics argue that shelter schools isolate the homeless even more, cutting them off from mainstream youngsters. In addition, as students move into elementary school, the shelter schools are separate and unequal, making them unconstitutional. Shelter schools cannot offer the same facilities —gyms and art rooms, for example—or the same educational content that a student could get in a public school classroom.

Although the value of shelter schools continues to be debated, other programs have met with widespread acceptance. Giant Step, a preschool program for low-income children in New York City, links the public schools with social service agencies and offers intensive support programs for parents. Testing results indicate that the program has had "twice the positive impact on children's performance on cognitive tests as other early childhood programs."[32] In Giant Step, the classes are limited to twenty children, and every class has a teacher, an assistant, and a family aide. While many other programs include a social worker, that worker is usually spread thin, serving as many as 240 parents. In Giant Step, every three classes have their own program director and social worker. What makes Giant Step so successful, most people agree, is that it links parents, welfare agencies, teachers, and the school. But it could not do so without being extremely expensive. The program cost $27 million in 1989. To budget that much money, a school system has to have a strong commitment to helping low-income families. It must be willing to finance the extra staff who are needed if programs like Giant Step are to be successful.

While new programs are one way to address the needs of low-income and homeless children, many individual administrators and teachers do what they can on much more limited budgets. It is not for lack of caring that the needs of homeless kids go unmet; it is much more often that they fall between the cracks because the schools and their teachers are already overburdened. Without the additional staff or the money for special programs that can help, schools can not be expected to reach the vast numbers of kids without homes. When they fail to do so, however, the chances for these children grow dim.

DROPPING OUT

Three of every ten high school students drop out of school. The drop-out rate for minorities increases to six of every ten Hispanic students, over five of every ten black students, and nearly five of every ten Indians.[33] In some urban areas such as Detroit, Michigan, and some rural areas of Louisiana and Alabama, the dropout rate is much higher, with only one out of every three students getting a diploma.[34] Two million students per year either drop out or graduate unable to read or write.[35] Many of them come from families with a history of homelessness. According to the National Education Association, the consequences for these young people will be a "continuing struggle to find work and to stay off welfare rolls."[36] The consequences for the nation as a whole will be $75 billion a year through lost tax revenues, the costs of crime and crime prevention, and the funding of welfare and unemployment services. "For every taxpayer, that means an outlay of about $800 a year."[37]

HIGHER EDUCATION

The unfortunate truth is that even when a young person manages to finish high school, his or her chances of going to college are becoming more difficult. Institutions of higher learning have for many years practiced "blind acceptance." They chose from the many applicants to their schools those most qualified, without regard to the students' ability to pay. If a student needed financial aid, the college then used the scholarships, grants, and endowments it raised through public and private donations to fund the student's education. This placed a definite hardship on the college, but it ensured that all young people had a chance to get an education if they were qualified. Recently, according to the *New York Times,* many colleges have begun giving preference to those applicants whose families can pay tuition.

Even if a young person is admitted to school with a scholarship or grant, colleges are open only two-thirds of a year. That means homeless students are on their own during noncollege time. Welfare will not help. Charlie is a nineteen-year-old homeless Norwalk, Connecticut, youth whose addicted mother deserted him when he was a sophomore in high school. For a time, Charlie was able to live in his grandfather's cellar, but he had to drop all of his sports and extracurricular activities to work to pay for his clothes and to buy his own food. His grades slipped from A's and B's to D's and F's, and by the time he was halfway through his senior year, he dropped out of school. Charlie worked the rest of his senior year, but he didn't give up. He went to summer school and got his diploma. By the next year, he was sure that he wanted a college education. But to be admitted to Central Connecticut State University, he had to prove to the admissions officer that he was both serious and capable. CCSU promised him that he would be accepted if he went to summer school at his local community college and got grades of C or better.

But to go to summer school, Charlie could only work part-time. Because he could not work full-time, he also had no medical benefits. For months, he suffered with a growing plantar wart. Standing on his feet in the bakery where he worked on the weekends was difficult because he needed orthotics, special supports in his shoes. He had no money to live on or to pay for medical treatment. What little he did earn had to be saved for school. When he went to Norwalk City Welfare, he hoped that perhaps for the next four years, the city would help him with a small food allowance and medical coverage. He was told that at nineteen, he should be working full-time or looking for full-time employment. "Higher education," his caseworker told him, "is considered something you can do without. Education is a luxury."[38]

In Charlie's case, as with untold thousands of other young people who have the intelligence and desire to earn a higher education so that they can make some-

This photo was taken by homeless kids themselves at the Shooting Back Education and Media Center in Washington, D.C. At the center, volunteer photographers and writers teach photography, writing, and media skills to homeless children. The program builds self-esteem among these youngsters.

thing of their lives, the present welfare system is set up so that it would rather they stay trapped at minimum wages with a minimum education than help them become strong, self-sufficient, tax-paying adults. It is little wonder then that many of those poor and homeless young people who manage to struggle through high school will find the doors to a higher education closed to them the day they finish public school. It is also little wonder that they will remain in or soon join the ranks of the homeless poor despite their motivation and persistence.

Unless something is done to arm homeless youths today with the resources they will need to be successful and financially secure adults, more children will face a life of homelessness and poverty in the twenty-first century than ever before in the history of the United States. Their problems will affect the nation as a whole in more ways than just higher taxes. Poverty creates its own set of problems, among them serious addiction to alcohol and drugs, prostitution, wife and child abuse, and other violent crimes against society. Yet, as we shall see in the next chapter, when our society fails to provide the education kids without homes deserve, we leave them with few alternatives.

CHAPTER 5
STREET LIFE

Homeless teenagers wind up on the streets because they have no alternatives. They usually come from one of four situations. Many were homeless as children, and their lives on the streets are merely a continuation of the lives they have always known. Some homeless kids come to the streets having fled the foster care system. Others are runaways, young people escaping home situations made intolerable by physical or sexual abuse. And still others are known as "throwaways"—children who have been forced to leave their homes and who have no other place to go. All comprise what most experts agree is "one of America's most devastating problems."[1]

An accurate count of the number of homeless youths living without a permanent home for days, months, and even years is difficult to obtain. Most homeless young people fear the authorities. They worry that if they are caught living on the streets, they will be forced into the foster care system or placed in the jurisdiction of the courts as "status offenders." While status offenders have committed no crimes, the fact that they are living without parental supervision legally requires the state to take charge of their care. Consequently, they enter the state judicial system, which may place them in juvenile homes. In many states, juvenile facilities are overcrowded, however, and kids without homes are frequently placed in other institutions along with hard-core criminals who have committed serious crimes. Young people usually want nothing to do with either the foster care system or the courts. Authorities, then, are people to be avoided.

Because of this avoidance, however, the figures available on the number of homeless youths are a best guess based on the number of youths who are known to be homeless. The U.S. Department of Health and Human Services estimates their number to be about one million.[2] Youth workers, however, believe that in the past three years, that number has increased to as much as 1.5 million.[3] Some believe the number to be even higher, perhaps two to three million. Generally, these youths fall into two categories: minors, between the ages of twelve and eighteen years of age, although some are even younger; and eighteen- to twenty-one-year-olds, who are legally of age, but who do not fit the profile of homeless adults. While many of these teens will return home, nearly 300,000 are considered hard-core homeless street kids, who will reach adulthood without ever again having a permanent home.[4]

Although by law the younger group of homeless teenagers should be protected by the states in which they live, the unfortunate truth is that the agencies set up to care for homeless minors often are not equipped to do so effectively.

FOSTER CARE

State foster care systems were set up to temporarily shelter children until they could be reunited with their parents. Sometimes children are given up to foster care by parents who are experiencing problems that make it impossible to care for their children. Sometimes, parents are homeless, unable to provide shelter for their children. Often the parent is a single teenage mother who finds she cannot support her children or care for them, but is unwilling to give them up for permanent adoption.

In other cases, the state legally takes custody of children to protect them from abuse or neglect, or when the parents' supervision is not enough to protect the community from the crimes some young people commit. Almost all foster care children come from families that are unstable and chaotic, and most of those families are poor.

Nearly half a million children are a part of the foster care system, and another half-million, many of them status offenders, are in detention centers and correctional institutions. Consequently, the foster care system is tremendously overburdened, especially in large cities. It is underfunded, too, and because there are too few social workers and too many cases, many times a worker does not even know exactly how many cases he or she has or where all of the people are. Social workers burn out easily under such circumstances. In Chicago, for example, caseworkers' loads have doubled —in some cases even tripled—in the last few years. Burnout from overloading caseworkers in New Orleans has led to a 100 percent turnover of staff.[5] With too many cases and a frequent turnover of employees, it is no wonder that children often get lost in the system.

While they should be protected by the foster care system, children pay the price when that system cannot be administered effectively. Examples of children whose lives ended tragically while under the protection of their states abound.

Nathan Moncrieff, bludgeoned to death in San Francisco by a male foster care couple in 1986.

A foster mother shows
two Amerasian boys how to cook.

One had a criminal record, disqualifying him as a foster parent.

Charlie Wright, age seven, returned to his prostitute mother three times by foster care workers, and finally beaten to death by her live-in boyfriend.

Henry Gallop, age two, died of mysterious causes in his foster home. Just over three months later, Aaron Johnson, a second child placed in the same home, despite the fact that it had a long record of broken rules, also died. Both died of poisoning.

Joseph Hout, age two, shaken to death by his foster father, who had hidden from authorities a 1981 conviction for rape and aggravated assault.[6]

While these are cases of children placed with strangers, other tragedies have occurred when children were returned to parents who were incapable of caring for them. In extreme cases, that places the children in extreme danger. Katherine Boo of the *Washington Monthly* detailed the case of Lillie Mae Ferebee, who was a ward of the state and lived in foster homes for over ten years. When Lillie Mae was fourteen, a Philadelphia Department of Human Services' social worker on her first child welfare case decided that Lillie Mae should return to her father, despite the fact that he had just completed a ten-year prison term for raping a child. Within three months, he had beaten and raped Lillie Mae. To make matters worse, when the department stepped in and placed her with a new guardian, they picked a convicted murderer who also sexually molested her.[7]

According to *The Christian Science Monitor,* these tragedies are not isolated cases. One has only to read the local paper regularly to know that the killing of children in foster care, the beating to death of children by parents the foster care system knew were abusive, and the sexual molestation of children in group homes are common occurrences. According to Congressman George Miller (D-California), "We are in the situation now where we are underwriting a state system of abuse. Amnesty International ought to take a look at these kids."[8]

While many foster parents are compassionate, loving adults who wish to help homeless kids, the problems with the foster care system as a whole make it a game of chance for children placed in its care. The lucky children will be assigned caring caseworkers who will place them in a supportive environment. There they will be raised by adults who love them as their own. Whether the system is working or not, those parents see to it that children have every opportunity to grow up healthy and strong. But the less fortunate children who are ignored by the system, who are placed in unhealthy individual or group environments, are not much safer in state custody than they were with their parents or out on the streets. It is no wonder, then, that many run away.

> *Once a child makes up his mind to live on the street rather than stay in the system . . . the approach to working with him has to change. He may be 16 and still a minor, but in his mind he has decided to control his life. He won't accept a very authoritarian program and he'll reject adult control over his life.*[9]

Les Brown, director of the Chicago Coalition for the Homeless, thinks that about half of the teenagers living homeless in Illinois are or were at one time wards of the state. Like the seventeen-year-old boy named Biz-Kit, many get so tired of being "tossed around between relatives and foster homes," that they take to the street, finding other kids like them:

> *I've been tossed around so much, I don't know who I am. Here, people don't judge you. You see things and you say, "So what?"*[10]

TEEN RUNAWAYS

While half of all teen runaways in the United States escape from foster homes, group homes, correctional institutions, or other state placements, many of them and most of the other runaways come from homes that are intolerable. Over a third of all runaways were physically or sexually abused by their parents or other relatives. Another 40 percent or more fled family crises such as drug abuse or alcoholism. One of every five ran from short-term crises such as illness, death, school problems, or divorce.[11] Many of them returned home, only to run away again, because the situation at home had not changed. Well over 80 percent of those who do go home return once again to the streets.

Most runaways who make the decision to leave home feel they had no choice. Sandy, described by Gary Turbak in *Kiwanis,* typifies that situation. When she was only six or seven, growing up in New Orleans, her father began visiting her bedroom. By the time she was eleven, she ran away rather than watch her younger sister experience what she had endured.[12]

TEENAGE THROWAWAYS

While in some cases, teenage throwaways come from homes similar to the homes of runaways, throwaways are forced to get out by their families. According to the U.S. National Network of Runaway and Youth Services, one-third to one-half of all homeless youths were thrown out by their parents. A U.S. Senate committee studying the problem concluded:

> *Families are throwing children out of their homes long before the youth are ready to leave. When they try to return, youngsters often find door locks changed and telephones slammed down by parents who are not willing or able to cope with them.*[13]

The numbers of boys and girls thrown out of their homes is about equal, although, interestingly, the average age of girls thrown out is fifteen while for boys it is seventeen. Throwaways come from every economic background and class, but unlike the rest of homeless youths, more are from white, middle-class suburban homes.[14] In more than half those homes, however, there is only one parent and perhaps a stepparent, and in most of those homes, a parent is an alcohol abuser.

Throwaway children seldom get kicked out over a single, serious argument. Instead, the family has usually had problems over a long period of time. Sometimes the throwaways have a history of behavior problems, and their families just get fed up with dealing with them. But that is not always the case. Sometimes parents expect far too much of their children, creating rules that are overly strict. Then when the child breaks these rules, they consider him or her incorrigible. Melissa was an extreme example of this kind of situation. One day she returned home from second grade to find her mother had called the authorities. Her belongings were already packed. "I just can't handle you anymore," her mother said. "You're naughty and you have to leave. I've called a lady to come and get you."[15]

While not all throwaway children are as young as Melissa, many times they have done little to be so severely punished. Barb, only fourteen, was thrown out when her parents divorced. Neither parent wanted her. Jim, just sixteen, argued with his father about mowing the lawn and found himself locked out later that evening. Mary's father found cigarette rolling papers in her room and threw her out.[16]

A few decades ago, situations like these might have led to a teenager's going to live with relatives. Families took care of their own, and often a grandmother, aunt, or uncle offered shelter when things became too difficult at home. Today, however, the extended family is a dying institution. Most teenagers who run away or are thrown out can't stay with some other family member until things cool down or until the problems at home are solved. Unfortunately, they have few other choices. They do not want to go to the authorities, for that can mean foster homes or juvenile institutions. They can seldom stay with friends for very long. What is left is the street, and it is to the street that homeless kids venture to survive.

When they first run away or are told to leave, most kids remain near their homes, staying no farther than about ten miles away.[17] Usually they can stay with a friend's family for a few days. But it is not long before the friend's parents begin to realize that something is wrong. Runaways also worry that their families might spot them or track them down. Fortunately, many times that does happen, and after a few days of living homeless, these kids return home to stay.

If they don't return home within a few days, however, they head for the larger cities, where they have less chance of being noticed. San Francisco and Los Angeles on the west coast and New York City on the east coast are "magnet" cities because they have such a large youth population and because homeless teens can easily go unnoticed. They hitchhike or arrive by bus or train, often with little money. Somehow, they

Runaway children are found all over the nation. This runaway boy is in Salt Lake City, Utah.

think they'll be okay in the city—that they'll find other kids and perhaps even a job to support themselves.

LIFE IN THE CITIES

What these teenagers really find when they arrive is that the cities offer little to help them get on their feet. The first thing they need to find is shelter. But in some states, shelters for minors are required by law to house only those who are wards of the state—in other words, those who dare to present themselves to the authorities. The authorities and most social service agencies to whom the kids may turn have one of two goals: to return the youths to their homes or to get them placed in the foster care system. While reuniting children with their parents is a worthy goal, both public and private child welfare organizations do not find it easy to accomplish. According to Jed Emerson of San Francisco's Larkin Street Youth Center, the response to "sixty-eight percent of our calls to parents of children who would consider going home [is] 'You keep the kid.' "[18] Placing teenagers in foster care is additionally difficult. Not only are suitable homes at a premium, but often, after so many years of problems in their own homes, teenagers are locked into behavior patterns that make it difficult for them to adjust to even the best of foster care homes.

Even when a youth shelter can accept a homeless teenager, beds are seldom available. For the 1,500 to 2,000 homeless adolescents in San Francisco, for example, only forty beds are available.[19] Youth shelters are always overcrowded, and because so many others also need help, a young person's stay may be limited to a week or two. Nor can minors go to an adult shelter. Adult shelters cannot legally admit anyone under the age of eighteen without parental consent.[20] While the laws vary from state to state, a young homeless person generally finds it harder to find shelter than a homeless adult.

Eighteen- to twenty-one-year-olds face the additional problem of being considered adults. Youth services agencies will not help them; they are not funded for this age group. Older homeless kids find that they are truly on their own. Those over eighteen qualify for the adult shelters, but the shelters available can be extremely dangerous. Young adults are easily taken advantage of by older homeless adults.

To survive, homeless kids turn to each other for whatever protection and support they can find. Cases in which groups of kids build their own shacks in the woods in suburban or rural areas or take over abandoned buildings in towns and cities are common. Sometimes they pool their money to rent a room for the night so that they can shower and wash their clothes. When they can't afford to do this, they bathe from the sinks in public restrooms or sneak into school gymnasium showers. Some become beggars, earning a little money to buy necessities by panhandling. They eat in soup kitchens when they can, or pick through the dumpsters behind restaurants and grocery stores for discarded food. Some will find a "Dutch Uncle," someone who takes them in, giving them food and clothing. But few will find a "Dutch Uncle" who will help them without expecting favors in return. They may find themselves being asked to do any number of illegal tasks—transporting or selling drugs, muggings and robberies—or they may be expected to pay for their room and board with sex.

Many homeless girls soon find themselves pregnant. The United States has the highest teen pregnancy and abortion rate in the Western world.[21] In Harlem, a district of New York City, 80 percent of all babies are born out of wedlock, many of them to teenage girls.[22] The majority of teen pregnancies occur among the poor and homeless. Many teen mothers were runaways or throwaways, left on their own to survive. Most will remain alone, trying to raise their children by themselves. They will be locked into poverty, and if they have children, they too will face the same destiny. Seventy percent of all poor children live with only one parent. Half of all poor black children have only one parent. These young people will become a part of the welfare system, and more than likely, will live their lives in welfare hotels. Equally likely is that their illegitimate babies will grow up as damaged and desperate as their mothers.

SURVIVING THROUGH PROSTITUTION

To homeless kids heading for the big cities, the cities glitter with opportunity. Only a few weeks pass though before kids without homes realize that the opportunities they dreamed about were illusions. Few knew that awaiting them at the train and bus terminals and on the streets were the only "opportunities" available—an army of people intent on using young homeless kids to make money through sexual exploitation.

A homeless girl will probably be approached by a pimp within the first few hours of her arrival. She may be spotted at the terminal, or while she wanders the streets, looking lost and scared. She is an easy mark, and pimps are especially adept at spotting newly arrived girls who will make good prostitutes. They are also very good at gaining a homeless girl's trust. A pimp will pretend to be a friend-in-need. Alone and afraid, homeless girls are vulnerable to this kind of approach.

> *A pimp sets himself up as a girl's rescuer. He talks softly, wines her and dines her, doesn't ask for*

sex, and gives her more attention than she's ever had before.[23]

The frightening fact is that eight of every ten homeless girls who remain in a city for more than a few weeks will eventually have to survive by selling sex.[24] Today, as many as half a million girls under the age of sixteen are prostitutes. Because they have dropped out of school and because they are either too young or unqualified for legitimate jobs, they have no other alternative. Many develop strong bonds with their pimps, who seem their only source of emotional and financial support. Because their pimp "guides" them, finding them shelter, buying them clothes, and seeing to it that they are "protected," many girls see their pimps as father figures. Few girls believe that they are being exploited. They remain loyal and obedient, despite the fact that their pimps are using them solely to support themselves and often to pay for their drug habit. And because many girls have run away from homes in which they were sexually abused by their fathers, stepfathers, or mothers' boyfriends, they have no desire to go home:

> *When you ask a teen-age prostitute if she wants to go home, she'll likely say: "No, I'd rather be out here doing it with strangers for money than staying home waiting for my mom's boyfriend to come into my room."*[25]

The same is true for homeless boys. About six of every ten homeless boys turn to prostitution. Many of them have also experienced sexual abuse. They hear from other boys that male prostitution is not that bad, that it is an easy way to make up to two hundred dollars a night. The supply of people looking for young male prostitutes, or "chickens," is as endless as the supply of kids on the streets. And because both boys and girls are soon drawn into the world of drugs as well as prostitution, many will eventually work to support their habits. Payment for their services is often in the form of drugs. Most kids hate "crystal dates," prostitution for a drug that will allow them an evening of drug-induced fantasy but little else. As one gay male prostitute told a *Newsweek* reporter:

> *You just want to make the cash to go somewhere and crash. But you're tweaking [craving the drug] and they give you speed and you think you're straight for a little while. Then it starts all over.*[26]

While they go to the city with hope for a better life, homeless kids seldom find it. Instead, they line the streets each night hoping to turn tricks. Patricia Hersch of *Psychology Today* described what she saw late afternoons and evenings:

> *I see female prostitutes, some as young as twelve years old, dressed in G-strings, stiletto heels and not much else. They're bizarre caricatures of little girls playing dress-up as they work to turn eight to ten tricks a night. Boys too young to shave are dressed in the most exaggerated stereotypes of gayness.*[27]

Girls may continue to prostitute for many years, although the youngest girls are the most in demand by those who buy sex. Boys find that the older they get, the less money they can make. Their careers as prostitutes usually end by their twenties. Many then must become pimps, or are forced to commit other crimes—selling drugs and committing muggings and burglaries, to name a few—in order to survive.

Many of these young people will be caught by the police several times before they actually go to jail. Prisons are seriously overcrowded, making it impossible to punish every offender. Those who do serve time will be placed in detention centers along with hard-core criminals, who will more than likely sexually abuse them. They will come out of prison even more likely to commit serious crimes than before they went in. Some will be placed in foster care, only to run away again.

Many of these young people will not survive. They will die from alcoholism or drug addiction. They will become depressed and commit suicide. They will sicken and die from malnutrition, venereal disease, or AIDS. Or they will be murdered. Many will die without a name. Between 4,000 to 5,000 teen and preteen unidentified corpses pass through U.S. morgues each year on their way to burial sites like Potter's Field. Others just vanish. No one knows what happened to them or how they died or where their bodies may be buried, if they were buried at all.

Although the federal government allocates millions to fund 343 centers across the nation, and additional millions for drug prevention programs for runaways, life for kids without homes is grim. Organizations whose goal it is to help teens do not have anywhere near the money it would take to change things, although they try. Covenant House, located in cities across the nation, and other "outreach" programs like it, continue sending their vans out each night to bring food and hope to kids living on the street. Sometimes they are able to persuade a few to leave the streets. Some of the caseworkers are even able to work with kids' parents, eventually reuniting street kids with their families. But unless society deals more effectively with the hundreds of thousands of kids who can't go home, kids without an education or the work skills that could pull them up from poverty, kids who need counseling and healthy role models to learn how to cope with their lives, the future looks grim indeed.

CHAPTER 6
SOCIETY'S FAILURES

The specific problem of kids without homes will never be solved until the United States government and its people are ready to attack the source of the problem. For the most part, homelessness is the product of poverty. Families cannot find affordable homes because safe, adequate housing has become too expensive. Jobs that once enabled low-income families to live in decent dwellings are scarce. The conditions in which poor families have been forced to live have created additional psychological and emotional problems that make it harder for parents and their children to break the cycle of poverty. Many have come to depend on the welfare system, and will live on the dole their entire lives.

The complexity of the homelessness problem makes solving it more challenging. No one seems to agree about what must be done. Some people even doubt a solution exists. But most experts do agree on one thing—the problem of kids without homes cannot be solved without addressing the problems of their families. And the first problem that must be addressed is providing a safe place to live.

PROVIDING HOMES FOR FAMILIES

Some experts believe that if parents could provide adequate, safe, and permanent shelter for themselves and their children, many of their other problems would diminish or disappear. For many families, this is true. Unfortunately, providing homes for everyone requires reversing the trends that have created the lack of affordable housing in the first place. This will be no easy task.

Many factors have conspired to create the housing problems homeless families face today. In many ways, finding and keeping an affordable place to live has become a grim game of musical chairs. Each player has in his hand a certain amount of money equivalent to what he earns each month. Some people have their hands full of money, while others have only a few bills. In the game, each chair is labeled with a price tag, but whenever the music plays, the price on each tag increases. At the same time, someone breaks into the circle and removes the chair with the lowest price tag, so that every time the music stops, the people in the line have to scramble to get a chair. Yet they can only sit down if they have enough money in their hands to cover the cost of the chair. So, as the prices of chairs increase, fewer and fewer people can afford them.

In the game, the chairs represent the rental housing market. The price on each chair increases every time the music plays. In real life, there are many reasons why rents increase. When the supply of something is greater than the demand for it, its value (the amount people will pay to buy it) decreases. On the

Until the housing situation in this country changes substantially, conditions like these will continue.

other hand, when the demand for something increases, its supply decreases. Consequently, people will pay more for it. The same is true with housing. The demand for rental apartments has increased, decreasing the supply. Consequently, the cost of rent has also increased.

The demand for rentals has increased for several reasons. One reason is that more people live in the United States today. In addition, young people who in the past would have bought homes cannot afford to do so today because house prices have also increased. Normally, the housing industry responds to the increased demand for houses by building more. By increasing the supply, home prices inevitably drop. But today many cities and towns block growth, construction materials and labor are costly, and land remains at a premium. Thus, more young people have to rent, and they have to rent for a longer time while they save to buy a house. Their need for rental housing consequently increases the demand. In addition, each time a low-rent building is razed or converted to a business or high-rent apartment building, the increased demand for the remaining apartments raises their value.

Unfortunately, inflation, the increased cost of things, lessens the value of every dollar earned. Each time the music in the musical chairs game stopped, the players should have been given more money. Most people at least get cost-of-living raises each year. Yet labor wages have failed to keep up with inflation. The real hourly earnings for production workers and the median family income have both decreased since 1979.[1] While in 1974 young families had enough money left over after paying their bills to save 4 percent of their earnings, by 1981 the amount they could save had already dropped to less than 1 percent.[2] In addition, because the supply of laborers now far ex-

In places like South Carolina, community groups are taught to build their own houses with the aid of low-interest government loans and teachers supplied by the federal government.

ceeds the number of labor jobs available, wages have dropped.

While these factors create the housing problem, others make the problem worse. They are the equivalent to the removal of chairs. During previous administrations, the federal government created many incentives that made it worthwhile for people to invest in and build low-income housing. Investors could write the depreciation of apartments and apartment buildings off their taxes, and tax-exempt bonds with low interest rates made it possible for builders to construct such housing and still make a fine profit. But in recent years, the government has rewritten tax laws and cut back on federally subsidized housing. As a result, low-income housing construction is no longer as profitable to builders and investors. Much more profitable is the construction of high-rent buildings.

In addition, many of those landlords whose buildings were financed by low-interest loans from the federal government twenty years ago will no longer be obliged by contract to keep rents low. Once their commitment to the government has been met in the early 1990s, many landlords will prepay their federal subsidies and convert their buildings to more profitable middle- and upper-class apartments. The eventual loss of affordable housing may be as high as 1.4 million units.[3]

Finally, many cheap, government-built apartment complexes are in a state of serious deterioration. Some, like Chicago's Cabrini-Green complex, have been compared to war zones, where violent crime and drug dealing have made the project dangerous and unlivable. The number of residents in Cabrini-Green has dropped from 20,000 to only 8,900, primarily because people are afraid to live there.[4] In some projects, the situation is so bad that officials have proposed tearing them down and rebuilding smaller units that will serve fewer people. Yet nationwide, more than 800,000 families have signed up for government housing. Some will have to wait ten years or more before their names reach the top of the waiting lists. Some will never get housing. Two of every three cities surveyed at the U.S. Conference of Mayors in 1986 had such impossibly long waiting lists that they were no longer taking applications.

Increases in population, the loss in the value of hourly wages, inflation, urban renewal, cuts in federal subsidies, and other factors have conspired to push the poorest people out of the housing market. In the game of musical chairs, each time the music plays, the prices go up, a chair is removed, and the poorest people are forced out of the game. In real life, the poor are forced out on the streets.

ADDRESSING THE HOUSING PROBLEM

In a survey taken near the end of former President Reagan's term of office in 1989, 47 percent of the citizens polled believed that homelessness was one of the most serious problems facing the nation. Why then hasn't direct and constructive action been taken to provide low-cost housing?

Part of the problem derives from negative attitudes that permeate every sector of society. Some of these attitudes are based on ignorance, others on prejudice or complacency. Some are based on fear. When Cardinal John O'Connor of the New York diocese of the Catholic church asked then-President Reagan why his administration had made no effort to build housing for the homeless, the president explained to the cardinal and his TV audience that "most of the people who live on the street are there because they prefer that way of life."[5] Perhaps it is easier to accept the fact that millions of people have no place to sleep by making it seem that their homelessness is a matter of choice. But almost everybody knows better. While isolated cases of people who refuse shelter do exist, anyone who works with homeless families can attest to the fact that they all would rather have a decent place to live, if they could afford it.

It is also easier to believe that the tax money and charitable donations expended on the poor, and the volunteer efforts that keep many temporary shelters and soup kitchens open, are going to change things. The best programs reach only a fraction of the homeless; the rest provide minimal safety and short-term relief. They do not solve the problem.

The only way to solve homelessness is to provide affordable housing. But when low-income housing is proposed, communities often create so many obstacles that projects are never completed. In *Rachel and Her Children,* Jonathan Kozol quoted a Staten Island, New York, borough president, who preferred the building of a new prison to house 4,000 inmates to the building of four homeless shelters: "A jail is preferable to a shelter because it's self-contained. It doesn't spill over" into the surrounding neighborhood.[6] Public attitudes toward low-income housing show the same fears. When a project is proposed, many times the residents of an area unite to fight it, claiming that low-income housing will hurt the neighborhood, real estate values will plummet, crime will increase, and the neighborhood will no longer be safe.

To exclude the poor, many towns have adopted strict zoning codes that require an acre or more for each unit of housing. In some areas of Westchester County in New York, for example, single-family homes must be surrounded by four acres. Ninety-nine percent of the land is residentially zoned, making it impossible to construct low-income housing without a zoning variance. When in 1972, a Nine Towns program to develop low- and moderate-income housing was proposed in Westchester, the communities banded together and fought the proposal in court. They won. County Legislator Paul Feiner told *The Nation:*

> *There is a silence here about the homeless. People in my district were very pleased when I came out saying let's help the homeless. But when I said I was going to support semi-permanent housing, I lost a whole neighborhood. Everybody wants to fund the soup kitchens. You have a lot of churches and synagogues involved in preparing food and going out to feed the homeless, but that only keeps them homeless. Nobody talks about the real issue —building housing—because nobody wants it built.*[7]

While not every town in the nation is as exclusionary as some of Westchester's towns, few people in the neighborhoods in which low-income housing is proposed are happy when they find out about it. Nor are all of their fears groundless. The huge high-rise projects that were once considered the answer to low-income housing have failed to improve the quality of life for America's poor. Instead, they have often intensified the problems of their residents, creating pots that can, in fact, boil over into surrounding areas. In the Scudder, Hayes, or Columbus projects in Newark, New Jersey, for example, one of every four apartments is abandoned or sealed. According to *Newsweek:*

> *Many of the drab high-rises have become free-fire zones where pushers armed with Uzis and .357 Magnum pistols battle for a 24-hour drug trade conducted in urine-soaked hallways. Those few tenants who have the courage to remain live bar-*

> *ricaded behind metal doors in fear of stray bullets, crack-crazed thieves and pit bulls. It is a world where the only way to draw police attention is to be shot and where deliveries are as rare as yellow cabs.*[8]

It is easy to see why many people believe that low-income projects might endanger their neighborhoods. Huge projects pack thousands of people into what one journalist likened to "modern-day Indian reservations," cutting the poor off from the rest of society with the goal of keeping them and all of their problems contained in one area.[9] Little is done to help good families and their children maintain a safe environment, or to give the residents the power to make decisions about rules or to enforce them. So many people occupy the projects that it is also difficult for individuals to develop a sense of ownership, and the consequent pride that comes from ownership.

In addition, many housing projects suffer from mismanagement and misuse of power by their managers. Ten days before a fire that killed eight-year-old Angel Jackson and her brother, the Chicago Housing Authority had forfeited a $7 million federal grant to remodel and repair elevators in their Henry Horner project. The firemen, unable to use the broken elevators, could not reach the fifteenth floor in time to save the family.[10] In 1988, another family of six, four of them young children, burned to death in the Desire housing project in New Orleans two weeks after city officials had forfeited $106,000 in federal money granted to install smoke detectors in the high-rise building.[11] The housing authority had the detectors waiting in a warehouse, but had failed to find anyone qualified to screw them in.

Unfortunately, even the best maintenance staffs are often overwhelmed by the huge number of backlogged complaints; they are too understaffed to fix the broken pipes or take care of the other problems that are a part of normal maintenance. To make matters worse, in some projects maintenance workers are a part of the problem. Often they are unqualified for their jobs, but are protected by unions, bureaucracy, and politics. In some cases, these individuals tolerate the drug trade and have been known to require sexual favors in trade for maintenance repairs. These kinds of situations can go on for years, because few low-income residents have the time, money, or power to fight back. When the situation gets bad enough, officials hire a new administrator and are "surprised" when he or she reports on housing conditions. In 1989, the new director of the Chicago Housing Authority called his department "the most corrupt place I've ever seen."[12] But it is unlikely that no one in city government knew about the situation.

Conflicting interests and politics have much to do with today's lack of affordable housing. The consequence of politics—lack of public commitment to programs, and prejudice against pockets of poor in housing projects—is that money that could be spent to solve the problems of America's homeless is often budgeted for more popular causes. Reporter Tim Unsworth noted in his "Shelter Diary" that Chicago has six small shelters for battered women and eighteen for stray dogs and cats. The city annually spends $28 million to care for the stray animals, but only $2 million to house homeless women.[13]

The influence of politics on the lack of affordable housing traces its way up to the highest reaches of the federal government. "There is an undeniable link between the Reagan Administration's budget policy and the dramatic increase in homelessness," New York Representative Charles E. Schumer told *America* magazine. A Media General-Associated Press poll found that

54 percent of the population believe "the poor are worse off because of [Reagan] policies."[14] While the executive branch and the federal government cannot conquer the problem of homelessness alone, little has been done in the past few years to fund housing. The federal budget for housing has dropped from $28.7 billion to $9.5 billion.

What President Bush will do about the housing problem in the first four years of the 1990s is as yet unknown. He has promised "a thousand points of light" and has called for "an enormous awakening" to the homelessness problem. He will have to overcome many obstacles if he is to reverse today's trends in housing. In some respects, the government has begun to respond to the growing demand of advocacy groups such as the Coalition for the Homeless and to recent polls which indicate that something must be done about it. But with low-cost permanent housing, as with emergency and welfare temporary and semi-temporary housing, a coherent, widely accepted philosophy and course of action have yet to be developed.

PROVIDING TEMPORARY AND SEMI-TEMPORARY SHELTERS

If the number of low-cost permanent housing units does not dramatically and quickly increase, society has but two alternatives. Either people can continue, as they walk to their jobs, to step over more and more homeless men, women, and children, or they can provide more emergency, temporary quarters to house the growing numbers of the homeless. But even some of the people who run public and private shelters for the homeless have some misgivings about creating more and better shelters. In his new book, *Crisis in the Streets,* Carl Resener of the Nashville Union Mission warns against "institutionalizing" the homeless to the streets. "Homelessness is not overcome simply by softening the conditions the homeless live in. The causes must be eliminated."[15] Many people worry that if a shelter system develops that meets all homeless people's needs, society will accept the shelter system as an established practice and custom and never make the sacrifices necessary to change it. Homelessness could become an accepted way of life.

Yet to effectively and safely house large numbers of homeless people, the shelter system must be set up to separate the mentally ill from families with children, and the people with addiction problems from those who are merely out of work. Providing trained staff to deal with people in crisis requires providing on-site health services. Each time new staff are provided to service specific needs, however, institutionalizing the shelter system becomes more of a reality.[16]

The institutionalization process could be hastened by building more shelters. Despite the fact that no one has ever proved it, many authorities fear that shelters act as a magnet. As soon as one is opened, it quickly fills. Thus in many cities, it is public policy that shelters must not be so comfortable that people living doubled up or in substandard housing decide they're better off in the shelter system. The shelter of choice, then, is the congregate, barracks-type so lacking in comfort and privacy that most people would not want to live in them.

There are people who worry that the U.S. system of welfare, paying for the housing of homeless families and attending to their survival needs, makes life doubly hard for the working poor. "In fifteen states, a mother with two children is actually better off on a combination of welfare and food stamps than working full time at a minimum-wage job."[17] Families in which one or both parents work are not eligible for any of the benefits—food stamps, a rent allowance, and Medicaid—that families in which no one works receive. Many experts worry that welfare creates a disincentive to work. If the wages a parent can earn provide less than the welfare money he or she can receive by not working, it is only logical that it is better to go on welfare. The numbers of those living well below the poverty level despite the fact that they were working increased 52 percent between the years 1975 and 1986, while the number of families receiving welfare increased only 14 percent.[18] Should the nine million people struggling to make ends meet without government help decide they are better off unemployed and dependent on the government for their living expenses, the cost to the United States taxpayer would be overwhelming.

Other problems with the present welfare system tend to "foster passivity and a sense of worthlessness." They are what Charles Murray, author of *Losing Ground,* calls "incentives to fail."[19] Foremost among these incentives built into the welfare system is the increase in monthly incomes awarded to those mothers who continue having babies, despite the fact that they can't afford to support them. According to Michael Horowitz, one-time aide to former budget director David Stockman, "The bottom line is that the state often replaced the male in poor families as the source of income and support."[20] This is probably true at least in one respect—the more children a single mother produces, the more dependent and "married" to the welfare system she must become if any of them are to survive.

DEALING WITH THE "POVERTICIANS"

"Poverticians" is a term that was coined in the late 1980s. Poverticians are people who profess to be helping the poor, but who, in fact, stand to make a hefty profit from their plight. They are in both government and private business. Crooked politicians can use their power to grant contracts to low-income housing developers or can lobby against programs that might jeopardize the money private interest groups make from federal, state, and local welfare programs. They do this for cash or for donations to their campaigns. Both practices are illegal. In the private sector, poverticians are some business people who stand to gain large amounts of money by providing often substandard buildings or services for the poor. Unfortunately, programs that help the poor almost always help the poverticians as well.

Examples of poverticians abound. In *Rachel and Her Children,* Jonathan Kozol cites many examples of poverticians who divert taxpayers' money into their own pockets. The most blatant examples are the owners of many of New York City's welfare hotels, but it is important to recognize that these people do not work alone. Often they have friends in the government who owe them favors or who are willing to look the other way. The Jamaica Arms, a New York City welfare hotel, had been seized by the city in 1982 because its owners did not pay their taxes. Instead of keeping the hotel as a welfare housing building, however, the city sold it to a private corporation for only $75,000. The buyers then resold the hotel for two and a half times its purchase price. The new buyers made an even greater profit by renting the same hotel to the city for $1.2 million a year. Whether by chance or by plan, the owners of the Jamaica Arms contributed over $100,000 to the political campaigns of city officials, several of whom determine housing policy.[21]

Unfortunately, while the poor seem powerless to fight back, opportunists, sensing money to be made off the misfortune of others, have leapt upon the spoils created by tax money earmarked for the poor. Another case was documented by two reporters from the *Washington Monthly.* Young Julian Summers, his mother, sister, and her infant daughter, cited in Chapter 1, are among the unfortunate residents at the Pitts Motor Hotel in Maryland. Cornelius Pitts, on the other hand, has prospered from the desperation of the Summers family and others. Fortunately for Pitts, when the Washington, D.C., authorities were looking for emergency welfare housing, Pitts had a "ramshackle" building that was once a hotel that he could offer. The hotel and the Pitts Motel now house scores of families and feed several additional busloads of welfare families housed elsewhere. The government's annual payments of between $1.3 and $1.5 million by 1986 allowed Pitts and his wife to drive a Rolls-Royce and a Mercedes Benz and to pull an annual salary of in excess of a quarter of a million dollars. Pitts managed to convince the city government to pay him $97 per square foot for property located in a "neighborhood of junkies and prostitutes," while select office space in town cost only $15 per foot. Worse, a local church had offered better services for one-fifth the cost.

Many poverticians are quite convincing when they talk about their "benevolence." Pitts told investigative reporter Marianne Szegedy-Maszak of the *Washington Monthly,* "It is difficult for a white business person to care for my people. I just don't believe that any white person can be as interested in the welfare of poor black people as a black person." City inspectors described Pitts's interest and level of caring: rooms crowded with up to six people, "loose plaster, leaks, poor ventilation, holes in the walls and floors, no fire alarms, broken lights, bedbugs, roaches, and other insects."[22]

While Pitts and others like him continue to play the system for all it is worth, despite the misery of those caught in it, it is not without the assistance and collaboration of officials that such situations are allowed to exist. One such official, the city's deputy mayor for economic development, was part owner of an apartment building that rented a furnished apartment to the city for welfare housing. The apartment cost $2,661 per month in a neighborhood where similar unfurnished apartments cost $350.[23]

Because of their welfare hotel and motel policies, welfare housing in places such as New York City cost more than they should. A member of the New York City Council noted that universities needing more dormitory space are able to find hotel rooms for an average of $355 per month, only one-fifth of what the city pays for welfare hotel rooms. Private welfare agencies are also able to provide cleaner, safer, and more adequate shelter to homeless families for less money. They also do a far better job of returning families to private housing in a shorter time. The Red Cross, the Henry Street Settlement's Urban Family Center, and Samaritan House find private housing for the families they shelter within four to eight months, while the average stay for the public welfare hotel family is thirteen months.[24]

Transportation is another area in which many people are making money from others' poverty. When New York City began housing some families in areas far from their former homes, children were forced to change schools. The state, however, passed new legislation that allowed families to choose where their children went to school. The law required their social service department to pay for their transportation. On the surface, a city policy that allows children to be taxied or bused long distances to their former schools seems benevolent. But taxis and buses cost money, often great amounts of money, that could otherwise be used to keep poor families near their homes. Sums as high as $1 per mile per child make it very profitable for private bus companies to operate. They charge as much as $80 per day per child for many of those being bused to and from city schools from distant areas. In one case Jonathan Kozol cited, a child temporarily housed in Poughkeepsie, New York, commuted each school day to Yonkers, New York. The trip cost $180 per day. If the cost of one day's ride was added to their welfare rent allowance, the family probably could have found an affordable apartment. One week's rides could have paid for an entire month's rent.[25]

Poverticians have been making great sums of money at the federal level as well. At present, the entire Department of Housing and Urban Development is under investigation. HUD has 13,000 employees and eighty offices nationwide. It was created by President Lyndon Johnson in the 1960s to provide a Cabinet-level advocate for those living in decaying urban areas. Today, HUD has a $20 billion budget, making it a target for graft, fraud, and influence peddling. Apparently, developers and builders paid employees of HUD and politicians who could influence HUD decisions vast sums of money to get government contracts. Sometimes they paid for these favors in the form of campaign contributions. HUD Secretary Jack Kemp asserted that HUD-subsidized developers contributed "the bulk of campaign contributions in recent Presidential elections."[26] In other cases, those who wanted an unfair advantage over their competition paid in cash. According to the *New York Times,* former Department of the Interior Secretary James G. Watt received more than $400,000 to contact HUD personnel on behalf of several developers who wanted federal subsidies.[27]

Poverticians undermine every effort made by honest government officials to help the homeless. Millions of dollars that could build new housing units, renovate old ones, or provide food, health care, or other needed services to help families become self-sufficient instead buy bigger homes or fancier cars for the poverticians. What is worse is that when these people are discovered and the media reports their crimes, it makes the public even more cynical about funding necessary programs. Either way, the homeless lose out.

Society's failure to provide enough housing units for all Americans makes overcoming homelessness seem nearly impossible. Yet the obstacles must be overcome. While finding a safe place to raise one's family will not solve all of the problems connected to homelessness, it is the essential beginning. Parents cannot be expected to be able to work on other problems until they have the peace of mind that a home creates. Children cannot be expected to seize the opportunity a good education can provide if they have no safe home environment in which to grow and learn. Nor can the United States as a nation begin to solve some of its other major problems—illiteracy, crime, and drugs—unless it commits itself to helping family members, both parents and children, take the first step toward positive, constructive lives.

The United States will have to enlist every citizen in the fight against homelessness. Programs to build safe, affordable housing are an absolute necessity. Plans to improve present federal housing projects need careful drafting. Profit incentives for private investors and builders have to be increased. At the same time, such programs will have to be watched to prevent more of the kinds of abuses housing programs have suffered in the past. In the meantime, the present emergency shelter system must begin to deal more effectively with helping people become more self-sufficient. It must remove the "incentives to fail" and replace them with strong incentives to become self-sufficient. Society must be careful that the shelter system does not become an institution in which the poor live out their lives; rather it should be a stepping stone toward freedom and independence. Many individuals and organizations are presently working toward that end. As we shall see in Chapter 7, excellent programs that offer kids without homes and their families a chance to change their lives are making a difference.

CHAPTER 7
DOING SOMETHING ABOUT HOMELESSNESS

While in most cases providing safe and decent housing for kids without homes and their parents is the first step to be taken to change the patterns of their lives, it is not the only one. While many experts believe that homelessness *is* the problem, recent studies indicate that perhaps as many as half of all homeless people are episodically homeless. Because they have been homeless more than once, other problems may well be interfering with their becoming fully independent. This is not surprising, given the conditions present today that foster teen pregnancy, birth defects, drug addiction, alcoholism, and crime. Nor is it surprising in view of the shortage of mental health facilities to help mentally ill teenagers and adults cope with the world.

Experts who believe that housing units will not solve the problems of the homeless stress that transitional services tailored to their specific needs must be funded. Some parents will need interim housing, perhaps a community mental health center, or a halfway house to prepare them to cope with their lives. Others will need intensive guidance and schooling to prepare them for today's job market. Some will need help learning parenting skills. For each type of homeless parent, specific kinds of help are called for, which makes the problem of kids without homes extremely difficult to address.

That "the majority of homeless adults have persistent personal problems," however, does not deem them undeserving of help. Rather, their problems make it all the more imperative that society do something about them. The growing numbers of kids without homes who will almost certainly grow up to be adults without homes if nothing is done makes the solution of the homelessness problem even more urgent. Because they are the fastest growing segment of homeless people in the United States, doing little or nothing to help homeless children is to allow the problem to snowball. Homelessness begets homelessness. Even more children will be homeless in the next generation, and more the following. Sooner or later, their burden on society could undermine the stability and safety of society as a whole. By then, their numbers may be so great that it will be too late to do anything about them.

Recognizing this, individuals, groups, and local, state, and federal agencies have mobilized to try to deal with homelessness on every level. Some are concentrating on supplying more affordable housing. Some are working on providing better and more effective shelters. Others have focused on developing guidance programs to deal with the specific problems homeless people tend to have. Other programs emphasize job retraining and preparing parents for the responsibility of full-time jobs. Some programs concentrate primarily on addiction rehabilitation, while others work with the mentally ill. Across America, civic organizations, schools, business organizations, celebrities, and the media are also working to educate citizens about the plight of the homeless. Others are doing their share by volunteering at shelters, in soup kitchens, and at other facilities for the homeless.

While the government is best suited to mount massive programs that require complex cooperation and large amounts of cash, the private sector has done an astonishing amount of work to help the homeless. In 1988, nine of every ten shelters were created and operated by community and religious organizations. Eighty thousand volunteers also donated their time to shelters, and an untold many more worked on short-term fund-raising drives. Although it may be true that U.S. citizens are worried and discouraged about the numbers of homeless people, they have not given up.

HOUSING PROGRAMS

Some private groups are finding new and cheaper ways to finance and erect low-cost housing. Commercial housing costs are insurmountably high for the poor for several reasons, among them complex and often elaborate designs, high cost of materials and labor, and high-interest mortgage rates. An organization called Habitat, started by Millard Fuller in 1976, has found ways to get around that problem. Fuller realized that housing units could be built for far less by volunteers using donated materials. Habitat houses are always simply designed, but adequate. Families are able to buy these houses at a price far lower than any on the market, and Habitat arranges mortgage loans at zero interest for them. Families are expected to pay back their loans within twenty years. Their monthly payments during that time are returned to the fund Habitat uses to build more houses.

Habitat organizations number over three hundred nationwide. All over the United States, people from all walks of life are involved in Habitat's building programs. Bob Montgomery is the director of research at the Blood Center of Southeastern Wisconsin. But as soon as he finished work last year, he took his toolbox —and often his two teenagers—to a deteriorated house in downtown Milwaukee. There, other Habitat volunteers such as Grace Morgan, a retired schoolteacher, neighborhood children, and high school students were renovating the building. Habitat volunteers offer all kinds of services—from carpentry and plumbing to writing applications for grants and zoning variances, from lending a truck to haul trash to donating necessities such as food, clothing, and bedding.

Habitat is one example of the large, national, nonprofit organizations working to help homeless families. Jubilee Housing, on the other hand, is a neighborhood organization operating in Washington, D.C. The first Jubilee effort was the renovation of two buildings in which garbage filled the elevator shafts and dealers peddled drugs. With the help of volunteers and many community organizations, Jubilee has turned nine deteriorating buildings into 350 units of safe, affordable housing. Each is managed by its tenants.

Jim Rouse began working to help homeless families with Jubilee, but went on to found an even larger organization, the Enterprise Foundation. Enterprise works with nonprofit local groups who help the very poor to build housing. Enterprise housing experts have studied ways to reduce housing costs by using alternative building materials, simplifying design, cutting waste space, and setting up nonprofit donated materials warehouses. Local groups that want to renovate buildings have been able to cut their expenses by as much as 20 percent with the help of Enterprise. In addition, the Enterprise Social Investment Corporation (ESIC) finds low-cost financing and uses federal low-income housing tax credits and loan funds from churches, businesses, and individual benefactors to help local groups reach their goals. When they receive help, many families are able to help pay for their housing through "sweat equity," working off their loans by helping with construction. The Enterprise Foundation has successfully raised $20 million in loans and grants and over $100 million through individuals and corporations for over three thousand units of low-income housing.

New York City's welfare hotels may have been the example of all that is wrong with public policy toward the homeless, but today the city's commitment to creating affordable housing is exemplary. According to *U.S. News & World Report*, ". . . New York is becoming a public-housing success story . . . on the cutting edge of a new urban commitment to subsidized housing for the poor and the homeless."[1] Because the media investigated and exposed the plight of the poor in welfare hotels, many of the hotels have been or soon will be shut down. Through a combination of private and government agencies, New York is renovating and using for low-income housing a large number of properties taken by the city because their owners have defaulted on their taxes. The ten-year program began in 1986 and will cost $5.1 billion. When completed, over a quarter of a million units of permanent housing will help to alleviate the homelessness problem in that city. "No city in America has attempted to build on this scale in half a century and no city has done it with their own money,"[2] Jim Rouse told *U.S. News & World Report*. New York's 1989 budget for this massive building and renovation program was $740 million, three times greater than all fifty other surveyed cities' budgets combined.

These are but a few of the programs now working to increase the number of available housing units for the very poor and homeless. Local church and civic groups that have witnessed their success are beginning grass-roots efforts to help members of their own communities who have come upon hard times. The Banana Kelly Community Improvement Association has redone more than 400 apartments in the Bronx, New York. The Mad-Housers of Atlanta, Georgia, began their "guerrilla housing" by building more than sixty "solidly built" wooden huts. They have now received a grant to build two bungalows in the city. Many efforts have begun as the idea of only a few people willing to give their time and energy to finding housing for homeless people. They have caught on, becoming the center of community interest. Although much is yet to be done to solve the problem of available housing, the work of these groups proves that affordable housing can be created when citizens and their communities join efforts.

IMPROVING EMERGENCY SHELTERS

Permanent housing is the best solution for homeless families, but transitional emergency shelters will probably always be necessary to house families until permanent housing is found. Temporarily homeless kids and their parents cannot be expected to begin to put their lives back together when they are housed in shelters that are degrading and inhumane. At the very least, they need safety and privacy and an environment conducive to rebuilding a sense of dignity. In the past few years, the federal government has authorized funds for emergency shelters. State and local governments have also provided money for emergency shelter. Yet some of the best shelters are the ones created and run by private organizations using federal and state grants and private donations. Many of these groups have already been mentioned in earlier chapters. The Red Cross, for example, leases a former tourist hotel in New York City to house homeless families. The city pays less than $50 a night for the families it sends there. The rooms are decent and clean, and each has a refrigerator, phone, and air conditioning. The Salvation Army's shelter in Houston, Texas, also provides private rooms and baths, and sees to it that all physical needs are met. "You don't see us on television much because we're not pitiful . . . it's the best, absolutely the best in the country," one proud director told the Houston, Texas *Chronicle.*[3]

The best shelters do much more than provide a decent environment. New York's Samaritan House, financed primarily by a loan from Citibank, has kitchenettes on each floor so that families can cook their own meals. Samaritan House also helps mothers find day care for their children and learn job and parenting skills. The House of Ruth in Los Angeles received a special grant to work with "high-risk" children whose families suffer from a number of difficult problems. They assess the children's needs and often provide therapeutic activities for specific children and counseling for their parents. The Good Shepherd Ministries, Inc., in Washington, D.C., cooperates with Jubilee Housing to get homeless families the safe, affordable housing they need to get back on their feet. Once accepted into the three-year program, Good Shepherd also works with parents to help them learn child-care and parenting skills. "By providing parents with both encouragement and accountability, we help create a positive home environment where a child's self-esteem can grow," director Gary McMichael told reporter Margaret Daly.[4]

When the local steel mills closed, a growing number of mothers—who had worked at the mills—and small children without homes in Braddock, Pennsylvania, needed shelter. Debra House was opened in the belief that "these women have the same goals and dreams as anybody else, but not the opportunities." The program's goal is to help the mothers who live in Debra House become self-sufficient. The same is true for My Place in Birmingham, Alabama. There the program links schools to families to help insure that their children continue to get an education in which their specific educational needs are met.

Jessica was lucky when her mother fled their rat-infested apartment. They landed in the Thorpe Center, where sixteen families are sheltered in a program run by Dominican nuns. Much of the emphasis in the Thorpe Center is also on providing the right environment for children and attending to their educational needs. Overseeing where and how they play after school, providing books to read, and a place to do homework are very much a part of the Thorpe program. When a child needs a tutor, school supplies, or even clothes to wear to school, the Dominican nuns see to it that they are provided.

Not every shelter provides private rooms. Barracks-type shelters are still the norm in many cities. Privacy in these shelters is a particular problem for families, one that many architects and designers hope to overcome using architectural tricks. Separating beds with 4-foot (1.22-m) partitions is one way to allow a family at least some privacy. Lighting that leaves strips of darkness between sleeping areas is another. Other people are experimenting with different kinds of furniture, hoping to find the right blend of comfort and indestructibility.

Thousands of civic and religious organizations that help homeless families have sprung up everywhere in the United States. They have taken as their personal responsibility the job of fighting homelessness and returning families to self-sufficiency. What they have learned and the programs they are designing have become models for new privately funded groups and for government-sponsored shelters. Whether the shelter is a 154-acre (62-hectare) farm like the Emergency Housing Consortium's San Benito County, California, shelter, where families may live for up to two months by helping to raise produce for the group's eight other shelters, or whether the shelter is an abandoned army chapel in Presque Isle, Maine, run solely by the rural community, new shelters are appearing everywhere.

EMPLOYMENT PROGRAMS

While having decent housing is the initial step families must take to become self-sufficient, employment for parents is equally necessary. Kids without homes are too young to work, but their parents must be able to find jobs if the family is to become stable. Employment can be a tough issue, since it is the lack of employment opportunities that landed some families on the streets in the first place. Many parents qualify only for unskilled labor; these kinds of jobs do exist, and they are a worthy means of employment. Unfortunately, in the places they do exist, unskilled jobs do not pay enough for a family to live on. To climb out of poverty, parents will have to have the skills required to find better-paying jobs. Programs must be provided to help them do this.

In New York City, a program called Ready, Willing and Able trains men and women to do rudimentary construction work. Ready, Willing and Able participants renovate buildings for homeless families all over the city. They rip out walls, ceilings, and fixtures, frame new walls, put up new plasterboard and tile, paint, and cart off rubbish. The nine-month program provides shelter and construction training, and pays those enrolled five dollars an hour. Those who graduate are promised a job through the referral network set up with help from the city.

Michigan has another interesting program, called LIFE, for Living in Family Environments. At present, LIFE is a limited test project that has proved very successful. Fourteen welfare mothers are being paid $21,500 a year to be foster mothers to severely disabled children. While foster mothers have to be carefully chosen for their sensitivity and patience, these women have had a tremendous effect in helping children who would otherwise be institutionalized. Many of these children have made great strides because of the personalized care and attention they are receiving. For the welfare mothers, however, participating in LIFE ". . . was enough of an ego boost alone just getting off the dole."[5] Their ability to help others even needier has built up their own sense of self-esteem, while the program itself saves taxpayers thousands of dollars—$10,000 for each woman on welfare and $73,000 for each institutionalized child.

Another test project is the state-supervised Self-Employment and Enterprise Development program in Vancouver, Washington. When employees are laid off by their companies, they are eligible for state unemployment benefits for twenty-six weeks, during which time they must prove they are actively looking for other work. With the new project, selected applicants are given SEED money in a lump sum to start their own businesses. They must take training programs in business feasibility, marketing, finance, and accounting, and must do the market research for their own companies at the library. In addition, SEED participants prepare a business plan which they review with a business counselor.

Other programs offer a variety of job-training plans to meet the needs of different families. The best shelter programs, for example, teach residents how to develop resumes, stock a "lending library" of clothes for job interviews, and develop a network of adult education and vocational opportunities so that every parent can find work.

PROGRAMS FOR HOMELESS TEENAGERS

The role of shelters for homeless adolescents has changed dramatically in the past two decades. A study completed by the Greater Boston Adolescent Emergency Network in 1985 described the serious problems confronting homeless youths today:

> *In the 1960s and '70s a network of emergency shelters was developed across the country to house an increasing number of "true runaways," young teens who had fled from a horrific home environment and had no place to sleep. From the phone booth on the corner or from a poster on a bus station wall, they were able to locate the nearest shelter and find a safe haven. Today, this still happens, but it is the exception, not the rule. . . . Due to the lack of other resources to accommodate and treat the chronic system youth, emergency shelters have become 30- to 45-day warehouses for adolescents with no place to go. . . .*[6]

Returning teens to their homes or finding them suitable foster care is the primary goal of all programs that deal with homeless adolescents. The longer adolescents remain on the streets, the less likely will be their chances of successfully returning home or adapting to a foster care placement. The first step, then, is to get them off the streets. This requires outreach workers to develop trust and to foster hope in street kids. According to the Institute of Medicine's finding, the availability of supportive services, rather than the provision of housing alone, is an absolute necessity for these young people. Many of the groups working with adolescents provide specialized services including birth control counseling, sex education that emphasizes unplanned pregnancies and sexually transmitted diseases, and drug abuse clinics, addressing the primary dangers faced by young people living on the streets. Covenant House in New York City has developed satellite programs in cities across the nation. Outreach vans wend their way along streets where homeless kids panhandle and prostitute each night. Workers offer sandwiches and counseling wherever they stop. Many kids return with them to Covenant House, where they can find shelter for the night. Covenant House has helped thousands of homeless kids to return home, to find foster placement, or in the case of older teens, to go on to get an education.

The Larkin Street Youth Center in San Francisco is funded by every level of government and by charitable donations. Larkin Street provides health and mental health services, runs an AIDS education program, and reports an excellent success rate in getting youths off the streets. Forty percent of the youths they have helped returned home, and the other 60 percent joined the foster care system. Other groups, such as the Nashville outreach program, the San Diego YWCA program, Bailey House in New York, and the Folsom Street Hotel program in San Francisco, are working to help the growing number of homeless youths nationwide.

OTHER CHARITABLE EFFORTS

Charitable efforts aimed at helping the homeless are mounted every day in cities across the nation. Some of them raise money, others donate clothing and food. Some are aimed at developing public awareness of the plight of homeless people in the hope that people will better understand the reasons for homelessness and the role they must play to end the problem.

Some individual contributions have been dramatic. They have attracted public attention and pressured public officials into taking action. Perhaps the most well-known homeless activist was Mitch Snyder, whose two hunger strikes may well have been the catalyst in getting former President Reagan to convert the Federal City College building into a model facility in 1984, and to prevent the government from closing it in 1986. For over a month, Snyder drank only water. By the time an agreement was reached, he had lost forty-five pounds and was in danger of dying. In a very different kind of activism, famous movie stars and entertainers, Robin Williams, Billy Crystal, and Whoopi Goldberg, run the successful Comic Relief, a show that provides both comedy and pathos about society in general and the homeless in particular. The money they raise through their personal appearances and through the shows have done much to help fund agencies working with the homeless.

While some contributors make the news, however, many more work quietly on smaller-scale projects. Students at Rollins College in Orlando, Florida, hold an Oktoberfest to raise money to feed the homeless. A toy store owner in Los Angeles donates holiday proceeds to two local organizations that care for homeless children. A furniture store in Milford, Connecticut, donates sixty rooms of furniture to families who moved from shelters into permanent housing. A family magazine uses its media resources to raise money from its readers and advertisers to fund grants to organizations helping homeless families. Tens of thousands march to the White House waving signs crying for help for the homeless. Individual and small-group contributions abound, making it clear that U.S. citizens will not accept the plight of the homeless or allow it to continue. While their individual sacrifices cannot end homelessness, they provide a strong voice that arouses other citizens to action. They make it clear to the politicians and the government that strong, effective state and federal efforts must be mounted, for only with both the private and the public sector working together will it be possible to end homelessness and provide brighter futures for all homeless children.

CHAPTER 8
PRESENT AND FUTURE PROSPECTS FOR KIDS WITHOUT HOMES

The Constitution, the Bill of Rights, and United States law guarantee all citizens equal opportunity to prosper and thrive. Yet economic forces can undermine those guarantees by making some citizens more equal than others. That is the case today. While the rich have grown wealthier than ever before in United States history, the poor have grown poorer and their numbers have increased. Their poverty affects every aspect of their lives:

1. They are unable to secure safe, decent housing.
2. They are unable to provide enough for their families to eat.
3. They cannot afford, nor do they have access to, health care.
4. The circumstances of their homelessness interfere with their right to an appropriate education.

5. They are incapable of securing employment that pays enough to improve their condition.
6. They have few places to turn for help.

A century ago Lord Acton, an Englishman who wrote about the United States, praised the American system, in which anyone who wanted to do so could better his or her life:

> *In a country where there is no distinction of class a child is not born to the station of its parents, but with an indefinite claim to all the prizes that can be won by thought and labor.*

Today, in the words of Chicago's superintendent of schools, "No matter what they [children] do, their lot has been determined."[1] Many things have happened in the last few decades to limit opportunities for the poor, but they are not the removal of constitutional rights. Instead, they are economic policies that have favored the affluent, strengthening their power, while at the same time "eroding the power of the poor, the working class, and the lower middle class."[2]

The "American Dream" has long nourished the hope of all U.S. citizens that the reward for motivation, perspiration, guts, and determination would always be success. Today, that dream is dying. As more and more families slip below the poverty level, unable to give their children the opportunities necessary to be successful, a new cultural inheritance may prevent them from ever changing their lot:

> *Their upbringing has in many cases deprived them of the inner resources to seize their chance, and they pass on to their children a self-defeating*

An enormous amount needs to be done in the areas of education, housing, health, counseling, and other areas, if what we see here is to be eliminated in future years: three generations of a family lined up at a church soup kitchen.

set of values and attitudes, along with an impoverished intellectual and emotional development that generally imprisons them in failure as well. . . . These poor are locked in the familiar pathology that, even more than poverty, defines the underclass: leaving school, out-of-wedlock teen pregnancy, nonwork, drug and alcohol abuse, welfare dependency, and crime.[3]

When people see themselves as helpless victims, it is improbable that they can or will take active, constructive measures to improve their lives. They believe that the forces that determine their destiny are far stronger than any forces they can muster from within to change their circumstances. When large groups of people share such self-defeating beliefs, they reinforce those beliefs in their children, creating a cycle that will repeat itself from one generation to the next.

That process has already begun. Louis Harris, a well-respected pollster, studied changes in public attitudes between 1966 and 1986. He found a growing sense of victimization among those he surveyed. Those who believed "the rich get richer and the poor get poorer" rose from 45 percent in 1966 to 81 percent in 1986. Those who agreed that "the people running the country don't really care what happens to you" increased from 26 percent to 55 percent. Those who believed that "most people with power try to take advantage of people like yourself" rose from 33 percent to 66 percent.[4] On all three questions, major segments of the American public seem to have lost faith in their ability to participate in economic development, faltered in their belief in the power of the common man, and increased their suspicion that they are or could easily be victimized.

The belief in upward mobility that fostered the American Dream is dying because it is no longer true.

While statistically it is true that the upper classes pass on to their children the opportunities and skills that enable the next generation to prosper, the same is not true in low-income families. Their standard of living has continued to slip, and their struggle to survive has become more difficult. Jobs that in the past enabled working-class fathers to support their families are disappearing. The jobs that do exist pay less in today's terms, and the competition for them has increased. Almost every expert studying present economic conditions has concluded that today's workers will have to remain locked where they are financially at least for several years.[5]

Economic strategists have long believed that the American system "is propelled by the profit-seeking of private investors."[6] Profit-seeking is thus a good thing —it generates more and more money. But it is the profit-seeking activities of today's private investors that have helped to create the army of homeless people now seeking shelter:

1. They have given new definition to the term "substandard" housing and convinced the public that substandard housing must be demolished.
2. They have torn down the single-room occupancy (SRO) flophouses and hotels that have long been homes to those living at or below the poverty level, and replaced them with more profitable (and increasingly expensive) high-rises, condominiums, and upper-class residences.
3. They have renovated or razed houses and tenements, gentrifying whole neighborhoods by displacing the poor.
4. They have used federal subsidies to build low-income apartment houses, but

as soon as their obligation to the government ceases, they convert those apartments to middle- and upper-class residences.

5. They have convinced the American public that building codes that require costly labor and materials must be enforced, thereby effectively increasing the cost of housing.

In the last few decades, as attractive new buildings have replaced dilapidated old ones, most Americans were unaware of the magnitude of the problems this construction trend would create. Gentrification brought with it higher real estate taxes for communities. It also cleaned out areas that drugs and crime had made unsafe. The newness, the shine and polish, the prosperity enabled people to continue to believe that "everything gets better in America." But things have not been getting better.

Today, the falsity of those hopes grows ever clearer as increasing numbers of homeless people roam city streets, sprawl in local parks, tent in recreational campgrounds, huddle under bridges, in alleys, in makeshift hovels, in condemned buildings, or on the doorsteps of those more fortunate. They are impossible to avoid. They are impossible to deny. As their numbers grow, so do their problems. As their problems grow, society will begin to reap the harvest of their desperation.

"We aren't going to get away with this. We are not going to get away with this. The 21st century is going to punish us . . ." Senator Daniel Moynihan said on the television program, "60 Minutes." He was not being melodramatic. Ten of the members of the committee that wrote the Institute of Medicine's massive study, *Homelessness, Health, and Human Needs,* felt compelled to write a Supplementary Statement to describe their reaction to the evidence they had gathered:

> *We can no longer sit as spectators to the elderly homeless dying of hypothermia, to the children with blighted futures poisoned by lead in rat-infested dilapidated welfare hotels, to women raped, to old men beaten and robbed of their few possessions, and to people dying on the streets with catastrophic illnesses such as AIDS. Without eliminating homelessness, the health risks and concomitant health problems, the desperate plight of homeless children, the suffering, and the needless deaths of homeless Americans will continue. . . . Homelessness in the United States is an inexcusable disgrace and must be eliminated.*[7]

WHAT MUST BE DONE— LONG-TERM GOALS

Eliminating homelessness and providing for the homeless children of poverty will most certainly be no easy task. Yet it is not impossible. Although homelessness exists in other countries and under practically every form of government, it does not exist everywhere. In Scandinavian and Western European nations after World War II in the 1940s, governments became involved in providing for the welfare of all citizens. Many countries created social housing projects that today make up a large percentage of all their nations' housing. By 1986 in the Netherlands, for example, 43 percent of all housing available was provided by the government. Sweden provides nearly as much housing, 35 percent. Homelessness is not considered a problem in these countries.[8] In comparison, only 1.5 percent of United States housing is government supported.

Unfortunately, many Americans do not share the same belief that the government should provide for the welfare of all citizens. Only a quarter of those polled in a 1985–1986 International Social Survey Program, for example, believed that it was the responsibility of government to provide adequate housing. Yet as the homelessness problem grows, the need for government agencies to take strong, unified long-term action and to deal with the housing emergencies that exist today is becoming increasingly clear. Local officials dealing on a day-to-day basis with the myriad problems homelessness creates have become especially vocal. "Many local officials grouse about losing federal support," Andrew Cuomo, son of New York Governor Mario Cuomo, and founder of "Housing Enterprise for the Less Privileged," told *U.S. News & World Report.* "But most understand it is time for them to step up to the plate."[9] Even the new federal administration has begun to realize the enormity of the problem and to recognize the need to end debate about the government's role in providing housing. Before he took office, President Bush called the plight of the homeless both a national shame and a national test.[10]

If the plight of kids without homes is to be corrected, the problems of their parents, and in a larger sense, the factors that create poverty itself must be dealt with. Doing so, however, will require a variety of approaches. Most of the following recommendations are based on the conclusions of the Institute of Medicine's report. Others are from the Supplementary Statement to the report, a paper not all of the committee that studied homelessness agreed to sign. A few additional recommendations are those of experts and advocates for the homeless.

Housing

The number of housing units available to the poor

must be increased. In the Federal Housing Act of 1948, the government accepted its obligation "to assure that every household has access to decent, affordable housing."[11] It is now time for the government to reaffirm its responsibility by increasing its housing budget, dealing with zoning restrictions that prohibit the building of low-income units, creating tax exemptions or incentives for builders and investors in low-cost construction, and reviewing building codes that increase construction costs. All children have the *right* to a stable, safe, and decent place to live.

Public housing should no longer be built on a massive scale. Huge, high-rise projects have not worked in the past, and doubtless will fail to work in the future. Instead, all new public housing construction should be built in small clusters in all parts of each city and town, including residential areas that have previously blocked their construction. Because small-cluster construction will add only a small number of people to the neighborhoods, they will have little, if any, effect on the quality of life, the safety, or the real estate values those neighborhoods have attained.

In addition, other steps can be taken to increase the housing stock available to the homeless. Before a family is allowed to become homeless through eviction by its landlord, a city government caseworker should be assigned to intervene on behalf of the family. If the family owes back rent, the caseworker should have the power to pay that debt or to make new arrangements for its repayment.

In every city across the country, vacant properties that have been taken by local government through foreclosure should be converted to suitable public housing. Cities should also actively pursue landlords who have refused to pay back taxes, taking them to court and seizing their property for additional housing.

Public housing that has been allowed to deteriorate should be renovated. The problems of drugs and crime that have dogged many projects must be addressed through greater security, tenant rule, and strict codes of ethics for all tenants.

The law that allows federally subsidized buildings to be converted to private apartments and condominiums after a number of years should be changed. According to the Congressional Budget Office, over half of the low-income units subsidized by two federal programs will become eligible for conversion within the next decade. If their owners decide to forego federal subsidies and convert to the private market, they will substantially undermine any progress the government might make by building new housing.

Food and Nutrition

No child should have to go without food, nor should any child's health be endangered before or after birth because his or her parents cannot provide the proper nutrition. Eligibility requirements for food stamps should be revised to include any families with children who are unable to provide for them, whether parents are working or not. To insure the proper amounts of healthful foods, the government must reassess its food stamp program and recalculate the cost of a proper diet in terms of current prices. Since many homeless families are unable to cook in the quarters provided by the government, a method for using food stamps to purchase restaurant meals should also be devised. Finally, those providing meals for the homeless in soup kitchens and shelters should be trained to provide a proper variety of foods to ensure that daily nutritional needs are met.

Income and Benefits

While children do not work, the employment opportunities available to their parents have a direct effect

Good food and nutrition are essential if homeless children are to break the pattern and have a better life. These parents at a shelter claim that much of the food served is either non-nutritious, harmful to children, or both. Some parents, if they can afford to, supplement shelter food by buying extra high-protein food for their children.

on the quality of their lives. The government must create ways to insure that working-poor families are not made homeless because the minimal wages they receive cannot cover housing costs. In cases in which working-poor parents are on the brink of homelessness or have already become homeless, parents should be eligible for allowances to cover the difference between 25 percent of their income and the actual cost of decent housing.

Families living below the poverty level, especially homeless families, require assistance. Many are unaware of the benefits for which they are eligible, while others find it difficult to get them. Information offices or outreach workers must make information about entitlements easily accessible. Public welfare offices should simplify the entitlement process, especially the requirement of a permanent address, which has in the past made it impossible for some families to receive benefits.

Health Care

According to the Institute of Medicine, "Health care is not the most significant problem facing the homeless; the lack of a home is. In fact, since the health problems of the homeless are both caused by and [made worse by] their homeless state, remedying the health care problems is only a Band-aid solution."[12] However, since homeless children's health needs often go unmet, several things must be done now to protect them against illness and disease. The government should create a national minimum eligibility standard for Medicaid that ensures access to doctors and hospitals for all children, whether they are receiving other welfare benefits or not. Clinics should be provided in areas where the homeless congregate; their doctors and nurses should be specifically trained in dealing with the kinds of health problems homeless people tend to have. Better means to obtain medication and other medical supplies must be developed, as well as techniques to ensure that medications are taken.

Education

Without question, one of the most important long-term goals to help homeless children is the provision of educational programs designed to meet their needs. Head Start and special day-care programs for homeless preschool children must be expanded to include every eligible child. When necessary, outreach workers must visit parents not taking advantage of Headstart and other opportunities to convince them of their importance. Schools must be required to identify, evaluate, and plan appropriate programs for homeless children in their system, including the creation of a communication network between caseworkers, shelters, and the school. Federal aid to schools should be tied directly to their meeting these requirements.

The federal government must also implement means for every child to get either a college, occupational, or vocational education beyond high school. Some colleges have recently ended "need-blind admissions," a trend that could in the long run mean that fewer poor students will be able to attend the more prestigious colleges.

The need for parents to continue their education is also directly related to their ability to secure higher-paying jobs. Means must be developed to end illiteracy and to train parents to become self-sufficient by providing programs that will teach them the skills they need to compete for jobs.

Social Work

In many cases, homeless parents and their families need more than housing, food, employment, and edu-

Programs such as Head Start have had a tremendous effect on the performance of homeless children at school.

cation. In families that are experiencing crises, whether because of the mental illness of a family member, drug or alcohol addiction or abusiveness, or whether the family merely needs counseling in parenting skills and health education, social services and support groups must be made available by local, state, and federal agencies. Only through this kind of intervention can the stability of the family be increased, their employment and housing ensured, and the quality of life for their children improved.

WHAT MUST BE DONE —SHORT-TERM GOALS

The short-term goal that must be addressed immediately is housing. Homelessness has grown to such an extent that providing housing for all homeless people, even if building and renovation programs began immediately, would be nearly impossible. In the interim, emergency housing will have to suffice. Much can be done, however, to improve the quality and quantity of the shelters that will temporarily house homeless adults and children. While many critics worry that making shelters too comfortable will attract more people into homelessness, no evidence has ever been found to prove that theory true. In fact, the best shelters that exist today also have the best record for quickly finding housing and helping homeless families make a successful transition from homelessness to permanent housing.[13]

In *Rachel and Her Children,* Jonathan Kozol outlined the requirements for decent shelter. The rooms or suites of rooms should be appropriate to the size of the family. They should have refrigerators and kitchens, intercoms, and a reliable bell system. Phones should be provided on every floor. Social services such as therapy for drug abusers, day care, preschool and prenatal programs, adult literacy and job training programs should be provided at the shelter site. Places for such activities as meetings, films, study, and recreation should be part of the shelter layout. In addition, Kozol states, untrained or manipulative guards should be replaced by competent security people, doctors and nurses should be available, and the number of residents should be limited to 100 families.[14]

ACCOUNTABILITY

Some of the most vocal critics of programs for the poor and homeless are quick to point out that the welfare system has created an increasing number of people who fully depend on the government their entire lives. Many, they say, wouldn't work even if they were given jobs. Even former President Reagan told a story about a California woman who picked up her food stamps in a shiny Cadillac. If costly programs to aid the homeless are to be funded, then it is only reasonable to expect that welfare policies must be revised. Disqualifying those who would work in semi-permanent or minimum-wage jobs only stifles motivated people. Additional allotments to welfare mothers who continue to have illegitimate children must somehow be tied to participation in other programs that will eventually give these mothers the skills to become self-sufficient. New, more creative approaches to motivating the chronically unemployed to work and to take responsibility for themselves are an absolute necessity.

In the meantime, kids without homes should not be held responsible for their parents' problems, nor should they be made to suffer hardships that will only ensure that they, too, will grow up damaged and deficient. While it may be true that their parents need long-term programs to change their lives, it will be the short-term programs mounted today that determine the future of this generation of homeless children.

THE COST OF THESE PROGRAMS

While it is easy to recommend what should be done, funding such massive programs will cost the United States taxpayer a handsome amount of money. While no accurate figures exist at this time, James D. Wright in "Science, Passion, and Polemics" estimated the cost at "some tens of billions up-front and several billions annually just to implement the housing recommendations.[15]

In his article, Wright breaks down some of the potential costs. If, for example, only one million people needed an additional $300 a month to help pay their rent, the government would have to allocate $4 billion per year to cover the cost. If the government attempts to build half a million low-income units, and if each unit's cost could be kept to less than $30,000, the necessary budget might be another $15 billion.

In addition, the federal government is in serious debt. The national debt, the money this country owes to others, is at least $140 billion. President Bush has pledged that at least $40 billion will be repaid by the end of his term of office. The United States must begin to pull itself out of the red if it is to maintain its place in the world market, and if the value of its dollar is to remain stable. Spending money faster than revenues can be collected has long been a problem, but the size of the present debt is compelling. Every responsible government official recognizes that the national debt must be decreased.

Increasing the minimum wage so that working families can afford housing would shift much of the responsibility for solving the homeless problem to the private sector. But the minimum wage would have to double to be effective. Prices of products would most certainly have to be increased to cover the increased cost of production. Businesses, especially those that employ large numbers of minimum-wage workers, would bear the brunt of such an increase. Many would find it impossible to stay competitive with foreign products. If the number of available housing units still falls far short of the number of people seeking housing, however, the increase in the prices of things might only result in ever-higher rent and housing costs. Worse, more jobs could disappear. To stay competitive, more companies would produce their products in Third World countries where labor is cheaper, or automate, eliminating the worker altogether.

FUTURE PROSPECTS

In view of the situation then, it is hardly likely that massive federal programs to house the homeless or to service their needs are likely to be funded. Nor is it likely that the government will force businesses to double the paychecks of their minimum-wage workers. "In the short run," says James D. Wright, "which is probably to say for the rest of this century, the focus will be on amelioration, not on solutions."[16] Public and private organizations will work to ease the situation and improve the lives of kids without homes and their parents by creating more shelters, improving their quality, enhancing the nutritional level of diets, strengthening social service programs, increasing access to health care, and developing better educational programs to meet needs. What they will *not* do is solve the problem.

In the 1959 Declaration on the Rights of the Child, the General Assembly of the United Nations pro-

HELP
STOP
HOME
LESS
NESS

claimed that "Mankind owes to the child the best it has to give." The framers of this United Nations document recognized that the future of any nation, in fact, the future of all nations, depends solely on the treatment afforded children. They recognized that nations that deny their children safe and decent homes, proper nutrition, medical treatment, and an appropriate education, are nations that oppose their own future. The people of the United States already see the symptoms of the disease homelessness has become—the illiteracy, the drug and alcohol addiction, the violence and the crime. Every day, more and more citizens are giving their time and energy to groups working to combat the problem. People with the foresight to recognize that long-term creative programs to end homelessness must be mounted *now* to prevent even graver illness in the future are lobbying all levels of government. Local, state, and federal government agencies have begun to respond with an array of programs, budget allocations, and enactments.

Whether in the long run the United States remedies the problem of homelessness depends upon the ingenuity, commitment, and persistence of its people. But most certainly, what this country does in this last decade of the twentieth century will determine whether the United States will endure the twenty-first.

SOURCE NOTES

Chapter 1

1. Joseph Berger, "Dropout Plans Not Working, Study Finds," *New York Times,* May 15, 1990.
2. "The Coming of the 'Couch People,' " *U.S. News & World Report,* August 3, 1989.
3. Melissa Balmain Weiner, "Homeless Children Struggle With Their Own Class Struggle," *Orange County Register,* July 2, 1989.
4. Claudia Feldman, "The New Homeless," *Houston Chronicle,* October 9, 1988.
5. Jill Nelson, "The Coming of Age of a Homeless Youth," *Washington Post,* October 12, 1989.
6. Marilyn Gardner, "Poverty's Legacy—Fragile Families, Vulnerable Babies," *Christian Science Monitor,* December 18, 1989.
7. Jonathan Kozol, *Rachel and Her Children* (New York: Crown, 1988).
8. *Ibid.*
9. James D. Wright, "Address Unknown: Homelessness in Contemporary America," *Society,* September/October 1989.
10. *Ibid.*

11. *Ibid.*
12. Kozol, *op. cit.*
13. Wright, *op. cit.*
14. *Ibid.*
15. *Ibid.*
16. Michael Evans, ed., *Homeless in America* (Washington, D.C.: Acropolis Books, 1988).
17. Wright, *op. cit.*
18. *Ibid.*
19. *Ibid.*
20. Gardner, *op. cit.*
21. Kozol, *op. cit.*
22. Gardner, *op. cit.*
23. "The Dynamics of Homelessness," *Children Today,* May/June 1989.
24. Kozol, *op. cit.*
25. David Whitman, "Shattering Myths About the Homeless," *U.S. News & World Report,* March 20, 1989.
26. *Ibid.*
27. Gay Talese, "The Homeless Woman With Two Homes," *New York Magazine,* October 30, 1989.
28. Kozol, *op. cit.*
29. Willem van Vliet, "The Limits of Social Research," *Society,* September/October 1989.
30. Whitman, *op. cit.*

Chapter 2

1. Brad Kessler, "Down and Out In Suburbia," *The Nation,* September 25, 1989.
2. *Ibid.*
3. Myron Magnet, "The Rich and The Poor," *Fortune,* June 6, 1988.
4. *Ibid.*
5. Tom Morganthau, Bob Cohn, and Monroe Anderson, "The Housing Crunch," *Newsweek,* January 4, 1988.
6. Frank Gibney, "In Texas, a Grim New Appalachia," *Newsweek,* June 8, 1987.
7. Beth Spring, "Home, Street Home," *Christianity Today,* April 21, 1989.
8. Morganthau, *op. cit.*

9. Claudia Feldman, "The New Homeless," *Houston Chronicle,* October 9, 1988.
10. Jonathan Kozol, *Rachel and Her Children* (New York: Crown, 1988).
11. Spring, *op. cit.*
12. Kozol, *op. cit.*
13. Miriam Van Scott, "No Place to Call Home," *Good Housekeeping,* January 1990.
14. Anne Fadiman, "A Week in the Life of a Homeless Family," *Life,* December 1987.
15. "On the Street of Broken Dreams," *UN Chronicle,* September 1989.
16. Pete Axthelm, "Somebody Else's Kids," *Newsweek,* April 25, 1988.
17. *Ibid.*
18. Suzanne Daly, "Family Shelters: Crowds, Dirt and Drugs," *New York Times,* May 8, 1989.
19. David Whitman et al., "America's Hidden Poor," *U.S. News & World Report,* January 11, 1988.
20. Feldman, *op. cit.*
21. Katherine Boo, "It's Not Just Washington," *The Washington Monthly,* January 1989.
22. Kozol, *op. cit.*
23. *Ibid.*
24. Scott Shuger, "Who Are the Homeless?" *The Washington Monthly,* March 1990.
25. Kozol, *op. cit.*
26. *Ibid.*
27. *Ibid.*
28. Ellen Tumposky, "Horror-hotel Scandal," *New York Post,* November 7, 1989.
29. Kozol, *op. cit.*
30. Fadiman, *op. cit.*
31. Kessler, *op. cit.*
32. *Ibid.*
33. Reginald Johnson, "State Funds 'Temporary' Motel Housing," *Fairpress,* March 1, 1990.
34. Kessler, *op. cit.*
35. *Ibid.*
36. James D. Wright, "Address Unknown: Homelessness in

Contemporary America," *Society,* September/October 1989.
37. Robert Coles, "Lost Youth," *Vogue,* July 1989.
38. James D. Wright, "Science, Passion and Polemics," *Society,* May/June 1989.
39. Kozol, *op. cit.*
40. *Ibid.*
41. *Ibid.*
42. *Ibid.*
43. Fadiman, *op. cit.*
44. Johnson, *op. cit.*
45. Kozol, *op. cit.*
46. *Ibid.*
47. Morganthau, *op. cit.*
48. Coles, *op. cit.*
49. *Ibid.*
50. *Ibid.*
51. *Ibid.*

Chapter 3

1. "Hard Choices Facing Low-Income American Families," *Consumer Reports,* June 1987.
2. *Ibid.*
3. Jonathan Kozol, "The New Untouchables," *Newsweek,* Special Issue, 1990.
4. "Hard Choices Facing Low-Income American Families," *op. cit.*
5. Kozol, *Rachel and Her Children, op. cit.*
6. *Ibid.*
7. *Ibid.*
8. *Ibid.*
9. Marilyn Gardner, "Poverty's Legacy—Fragile Families, Vulnerable Babies," *Christian Science Monitor,* December 18, 1989.
10. *Ibid.*
11. *Ibid.*
12. *Ibid.*
13. *Ibid.*
14. Kozol, *Rachel and Her Children, op. cit.*

15. *Ibid.*
16. Gardner, *op. cit.*
17. *Ibid.*
18. Miriam Van Scott, "No Place to Call Home," *Good Housekeeping,* January 1990.
19. Kozol, *Rachel and Her Children, op. cit.*
20. *Ibid.*
21. *Ibid.*
22. John McCormick, "America's Third World," *Newsweek,* August 8, 1988.
23. Kozol, *Rachel and Her Children, op. cit.*
24. Institute of Medicine, *Homelessness, Health, and Human Needs* (Washington, D.C.: National Academy Press, 1988).
25. "The Unhealthy Homeless," *The Futurist,* July/August 1989.
26. Institute of Medicine, *op. cit.*
27. "The Children of the Homeless," *U.S. News & World Report,* August 3, 1987.
28. *Ibid.*
29. Kozol, *Rachel and Her Children, op. cit.*
30. Colleen O'Connor, Andrew Murr, and Pat Wingert, "Affluent America's Forgotten Children,"
31. Gardner, *op. cit.*
32. Patricia Hersch, "Coming of Age on City Streets," *Psychology Today,* January 1988.
33. *Ibid.*
34. *Ibid.*
35. *Ibid.*
36. *Ibid.*
37. *Ibid.*
38. Pete Axthelm, "Somebody Else's Kids," *Newsweek,* April 25, 1988.
39. *Ibid.*
40. Hersch, *op. cit.*
41. Gary Turbak, "Born, Raised . . . Thrown Away," *Kiwanis,* November/December 1988.
42. "The New Poor: Jobless and Homeless in the United States," *The Futurist,* March/April 1986.

Chapter 4

1. Jonathan Kozol, "The New Untouchables," *Newsweek,* Special Issue, 1990.
2. E. Anne Eddowes and John R. Hranitz, "Educating Children of the Homeless," *Educational Digest,* October 1989.
3. Connie Leslie et al., "Can a Shelter Be a School?," *Newsweek,* January 23, 1989.
4. Jonathan Kozol, *Rachel and Her Children* (New York: Crown, 1988).
5. Melissa Balmain Weiner, "Homeless Children Struggle With Their Own Class Struggle," *Orange County Register,* July 2, 1989.
6. Kozol, "The New Untouchables," *op. cit.*
7. Fred M. Hechinger, "About Education," *New York Times,* March 14, 1990.
8. Joseph Berger, "Dropout Plans Not Working, Study Finds," *New York Times,* May 15, 1990.
9. Hechinger, *op. cit.*
10. Berger, *op. cit.*
11. Weiner, *op. cit.*
12. *Ibid.*
13. *Ibid.*
14. *Ibid.*
15. *Ibid.*
16. Leslie, *op. cit.*
17. Hechinger, *op. cit.*
18. Weiner, *op. cit.*
19. Leslie, *op. cit.*
20. Berger, *op. cit.*
21. *Ibid.*
22. Joseph Berger, "Homeless Children Find Refuge In Their School," *New York Times,* April 11, 1990.
23. Berger, *op. cit.*
24. "The Coming of the 'Couch People,' " *U.S. News & World Report,* August 7, 1989.
25. Kozol, *Rachel and Her Children, op. cit.*
26. Kozol, "The New Untouchables," *op. cit.*
27. Miriam Horn, "The Burgeoning of the Educational Underclass," *U.S. News & World Report,* May 18, 1987.

28. *Ibid.*
29. *Ibid.*
30. *Ibid.*
31. Kim Moyer, "Schools for the Homeless," *Educational Digest,* February 1990.
32. Stuart Wells, "Preschool Program in New York Reported to Surpass Head Start," *New York Times,* May 16, 1990.
33. Ronaleen R. Roha, "What It's Like To Help The Homeless," *Changing Times,* July 1989.
34. Horn, *op. cit.*
35. *Ibid.*
36. *Ibid.*
37. *Ibid.*
38. Interview with Martha MacDonald, Norwalk, Connecticut, City Welfare Department, May 26, 1990.

Chapter 5

1. Gary Turbak, "Born, Raised . . . Thrown Away," *Kiwanis,* November/December 1988.
2. *Ibid.*
3. A. Dahleen Glanton, "Homeless Kids: Biggest Challenge Is Staying Alive," *Chicago Tribune,* December 17, 1989.
4. Patricia Hersch, "Coming of Age on City Streets," *Psychology Today,* January 1988.
5. Cheryl Sullivan, "Foster Care Doesn't Guarantee Safety," *Christian Science Monitor,* September 27, 1988.
6. *Ibid.*
7. Katherine Boo, "It's Not Just Washington," *Washington Monthly,* January 1989.
8. Sullivan, *op. cit.*
9. Turbak, *op. cit.*
10. *Ibid.*
11. Hersch, *op. cit.*
12. *Ibid.*
13. Turbak, *op. cit.*
14. Glanton, *op. cit.*
15. Turbak, *op. cit.*
16. *Ibid.*

17. *Ibid.*
18. Pete Axthelm, "Somebody Else's Kids," *Newsweek*, April 25, 1988.
19. *Ibid.*
20. Turbak, *op. cit.*
21. Colleen O'Connor, Andrew Murr, and Pat Wingert, "Affluent America's Forgotten Children,"
22. Myron Magnet, "The Rich and The Poor," *Fortune*, June 6, 1988.
23. Turbak, *op. cit.*
24. *Ibid.*
25. *Ibid.*
26. Axthelm, *op. cit.*
27. Hersch, *op. cit.*

Chapter 6

1. David M. Gordon, "The Ability To Provide Is Eroding," *Washington Post*,
2. *Ibid.*
3. Richard P. Appelbaum, "The Affordability Gap," *Society*, May/June 1989.
4. Tom Morganthau, Bob Cohn, and Monroe Anderson, "The Housing Crunch," *Newsweek*, January 4, 1988.
5. Calvin Trillin, "Uncivil Liberties," *The Nation*, February 13, 1989.
6. Jonathan Kozol, *Rachel and Her Children* (New York: Crown, 1988).
7. Brad Kessler, "Down and Out in Suburbia," *The Nation*, September 25, 1989.
8. Morganthau, *op. cit.*
9. *Ibid.*
10. Katherine Boo, "It's Not Just Washington," *Washington Monthly*, January 1989.
11. *Ibid.*
12. *Ibid.*
13. Tim Unsworth, "Shelter Diary: Help Me Make It Through The Night," *U.S. Catholic*, February 1990.
14. "Rays of Hope For the Homeless," *America*, January 14, 1989.

15. Beth Spring, "Home, Street Home," *Christianity Today,* April 21, 1989.
16. Russell K. Schutt, "Objectivity Versus Outrage," *Society,* May/June 1989.
17. David Whitman et al., "America's Hidden Poor," *U.S. News & World Report,* January 11, 1988.
18. Colleen O'Connor, Andrew Murr, and Pat Wingert, "Affluent America's Forgotten Children,"
19. Myron Magnet, "The Rich and The Poor," *Fortune,* June 6, 1988.
20. O'Connor, *op. cit.*
21. Kozol, *Rachel and Her Children, op. cit.*
22. Boo, *op. cit.*
23. *Ibid.*
24. Kozol, *Rachel and Her Children, op. cit.*
25. *Ibid.*
26. Clifford D. May, "How HUD Helped Many Make Money From Poverty," *New York Times,* June 25, 1989.
27. *Ibid.*

Chapter 7

1. Scott Minerbrook, "The Big-City Push to Fill the Housing Gap for the Poor," *U.S. News & World Report,* August 28/September 4, 1989.
2. *Ibid.*
3. Claudia Feldman, "The New Homeless," *Houston Chronicle,* October 9, 1988.
4. Margaret Daly, "Homeless Families in America," *Better Homes and Gardens,* December 1989.
5. Louis Aguilar, "Helping Their Way Off Welfare," *Time,* May 7, 1990.
6. Institute of Medicine, *Homelessness, Health, and Human Needs* (Washington, D.C.: National Academy Press, 1988).

Chapter 8

1. Jonathan Kozol, "The New Untouchables," *Newsweek,* Special Issue, 1990.

2. David M. Gordon, "The Ability To Provide Is Eroding," *Washington Post.*
3. Myron Magnet, "The Rich and The Poor," *Fortune,* June 6, 1988.
4. Gordon, *op. cit.*
5. *Ibid.*
6. Willem van Vliet, "The Limits of Social Research," *Society,* September/October 1989.
7. Institute of Medicine, *Homelessness, Health, and Human Needs* (Washington, D.C.: National Academy Press, 1988).
8. Van Vliet, *op. cit.*
9. Scott Minerbrook, "The Big-City Push to Fill the Housing Gap for the Poor," *U.S. News & World Report,* August 28/September 4, 1989.
10. "Rays of Hope For the Homeless," *America,* January 14, 1989.
11. Drew Altman et al., "Health Care for the Homeless," *Society,* May/June 1989.
12. Institute of Medicine, *op. cit.*
13. Jonathan Kozol, *Rachel and Her Children* (New York: Crown, 1988).
14. *Ibid.*
15. James D. Wright, "Science, Passion and Polemics," *Society,* May/June 1989.
16. James D. Wright, "Address Unknown: Homelessness in Contemporary America," *Society,* September/October 1989.

BIBLIOGRAPHY

BOOKS

Beckelman, Laurie. *The Homeless.* New York: Crestwood House, 1989.

Dudley, William, ed. *Poverty: Opposing Viewpoints.* St. Paul, Minn.: Greenhaven Press, 1988.

Evans, Michael A. W., ed. *Homeless in America.* Washington, D.C.: Acropolis Books, 1988.

Hirsch, Kathleen. *Songs From the Alley.* New York: Ticknor & Fields, 1989.

Hollyman, Stephania. *We the Homeless: Portraits of America's Displaced Persons.* New York: Philosophical Library, 1988.

Hombs, Mary Ellen, and Mitch Snyder. *Homelessness in America.* Washington, D.C.: The Community for Creative Non-Violence, 1982.

Hyde, Margaret O. *The Homeless.* Hillside, N.J.: Enslow Publishers, 1989.

Institute of Medicine. *Homelessness, Health, and Human Needs.* Washington, D.C.: National Academy Press, 1988.

Kates, Brian. *The Murder of a Shopping Bag Lady.* New York: Harcourt, Brace, Jovanovich, 1985.

Kozol, Jonathan. *Rachel and Her Children.* New York: Crown Publisher, 1988.

Momen, Jamshid A., ed. *Homelessness in the United States.* New York: Greenwood Press, 1989.

Nordquist, Joan. *The Homeless in America.* Santa Cruz, Calif.: Reference & Research Services, 1988.

Rosseau, Anne Marie. *Shopping Bag Ladies.* New York: Pilgrim Press, 1981.

Rossi, Peter H. *Down and Out in America.* Chicago: University of Chicago Press, 1989.

Trager, Oliver, ed. *Poverty in America: The Forgotten Millions.* New York: Facts on File, 1989.

Wright, James D. *Address Unknown: The Homeless in America.* Hawthorne, N.Y.: de Gruyter, 1989.

MAGAZINES AND NEWSPAPERS

Adler, Jerry, Lynn Davenport, Jeanne Gordon, Daniel Glick, and Roxie Hammill. "New Shapes in Shelters." *Newsweek,* January 1, 1990.

Aguilar, Louis. "Helping Their Way Off Welfare." *Time,* May 7, 1990.

Altman, Drew, Ellen L. Bassuk, William R. Breakey, A. Alan Fischer, Charles R. Halpern, Gloria Smith, Nathan Stark, Bruce Vladeck, and Phyllis Wolfe. "Health Care For the Homeless." *Society,* May/June, 1989.

Anderson, George M. "Defending the Poor: A Harder Task." *America,* January 14, 1989.

Appelbaum, Richard P. "The Affordability Gap." *Society,* May/June 1989.

Axthelm, Pete. "Somebody Else's Kids." *Newsweek,* April 25, 1988.

Bader, Eleanor J. "The 'Housing Now!' March on Washington." *The Humanist,* January/February 1990.

Bates, Lincoln S. "Mad Housers Help Homeless." *The Progressive,* February 10, 1989.

Bauman, Mark and Patrice O'Shaughnessy. "City Dismantles Shanties in Tompkins Park." *New York Daily News,* November 7, 1989.

Berger, Joseph. "Dropout Plans Not Working, Study Finds." *New York Times,* May 15, 1990.

———. "Homeless Children Find Refuge in Their School." *New York Times,* April 11, 1990.

———. "When School Offers Refuge to Homeless." *New York Times,* April 9, 1990.

Boo, Katherine. "It's Not Just Washington." *The Washington Monthly,* January 1989.

Brozan, Nadine. "From Citibank, Millions for Schools." *New York Times,"* May 16, 1990.

Bruno, C.C. "Why I Am Homeless." *Humanist,* May/June 1989.

"The Children of the Homeless." *U.S. News & World Report,* August 3, 1987.

Chira, Susan. "Smith Decision on Student Aid: 'Tip of the Iceberg'." *New York Times,* May 16, 1990.

Claitor, Diana. "The Homeless Take to the Water." *The Progressive,* February 10, 1989.

Coles, Robert. "Lost Youth." *Vogue,* July 1989.

"The Coming of the 'Couch People'." *U.S. News & World Report,* August 3, 1989.

"The Court Rules for the Homeless." *New York Times,* April 6, 1990.

Daly, Margaret. "Helping Homeless Families." *Better Homes and Gardens,* September 1989.

———. "Homeless Families in America." *Better Homes and Gardens,* December 1989.

Daly, Suzanne. "Family Shelters: Crowds, Dirt and Drugs." *New York Times,* May 8, 1989.

"Despite Problems, The Census Bureau Hails Its First Count of the Homeless." *New York Times,* March 22, 1990.

"The Dynamics of Homelessness." *Children Today,* May/June 1989.

Eddowes, E. Anne and John R. Hranitz. "Educating Children of the Homeless." *Educational Digest,* October 1989.

"Equivalency Degrees Down." *New York Times,* May 16, 1990.

Fadiman, Anne. "A Week in the Life of a Homeless Family." *Life,* December 1987.

Feldman, Claudia. "The New Homeless." *Houston Chronicle,* October 9, 1988.

Finder, Alan. "Homeless, They Build For Peers." *New York Times,* March 12, 1990.

Fleischer, Leonore. "Talk of the Trade." *Publishers Weekly,* January 27, 1989.

Gibney, Frank. "In Texas, A Grim New Appalachia." *Newsweek,* June 8, 1987.

Gardner, Marilyn. "Poverty's Legacy—Fragile Families, Vulnerable Babies." *Christian Science Monitor,* December 18, 1989.

Glanton, A. Dahleen. "Homeless Kids: Biggest Challenge Is Staying Alive." *Chicago Tribune,* December 17, 1989.

Gilden, Julia. "See How They Run." *In These Times,* December 20, 1989–January 9, 1990.

Golden, Tim. "Ill, Possibly Violent, and No Place to Go." *New York Times,* April 2, 1990.

———. "No More Room in the Budget For the Homeless Mentally Ill." *New York Times,* April 15, 1990.

Gordon, David M. "The Ability To Provide Is Eroding." *Washington Post.*

Hackett, George and Peter McKillop. "A Nightmare on 42nd Street." *Newsweek,* February 27, 1989.

Hall, Trish. "Tackling Homelessness Close to Home." *New York Times,* October 31, 1989.

"Hard Choices Facing Low-Income American Families." *Consumer Reports,* June 1987.

Harvey, F. Barton. "A New Enterprise." *Humanist,* May/June 1989.

Hechinger, Fred M. "About Education." *New York Times,* March 14, 1990.

Hersch, Patricia. "Coming of Age on City Streets." *Psychology Today,* January 1988.

Hoch, Charles. "When Scientists Dissent." *Society,* May/June 1989.

"Homeless in Capital Sue Over Hotels." *New York Times,* February 13, 1990.

"Homelessness, A Humanist Response." *Humanist,* May/June 1989.

Horn, Miriam. "The Burgeoning of the Educational Underclass." *U.S. News & World Report,* May 18, 1987.

"How Not to Help the Homeless." *U.S. News & World Report,* August 28/September 4, 1989.

Johnson, Reginal. "State Funds 'Temporary' Motel Housing." *Fairpress,* March 1, 1990.

Kessler, Brad. "Down and Out in Suburbia." *The Nation,* September 25, 1989.

Kilborn, Peter T. "Novel Program for the Jobless Aims to Create Entrepreneurs." *New York Times,* May 16, 1990.

King, Charles F. "Homelessness in America." *Humanist,* May/June 1989.

Kozol, Jonathan. "The New Untouchables." *Newsweek,* Special Issue, 1990.

Lave, Judith R. "Band-Aid Solutions." *Society,* May/June 1989.

Leo, John. "Homeless Rights, Community Wrongs." *U.S. News & World Report,* July 24, 1989.

Leslie, Connie, Pamela Abramson, Kate Robins, and Tessa Namuth. "Can a Shelter Be a School?" *Newsweek,* January 23, 1989.

McAnally, Gene. "I Was Homeless." *Humanist,* May/June 1989.

McCormick, John. "America's Third World." *Newsweek,* August 8, 1988.

Magnet, Myron. "The Rich and the Poor." *Fortune,* June 6, 1988.

Matthews, Richard. "A Tragic Harvest." *Country Journal,* September/October 1989.

May, Clifford D. "How HUD Helped Many Make Money From Poverty." *New York Times,* June 25, 1989.

Minerbrook, Scott. "The Big-City Push to Fill the Housing Gap for the Poor." *U.S. News & World Report,* August 28/September 4, 1989.

Mooney, Mark. "City Ousts 17 Homeless at City Hall Shantytown." *New York Post,* April 5, 1990.

Morganthau, Tom. "Children of the Underclass." *Newsweek,* September 11, 1989.

Morganthau, Tom, Bob Cohn, and Monroe Anderson. "The Housing Crunch." *Newsweek,* January 4, 1988.

Moyer, Kim. "Schools for the Homeless." *Educational Digest,* February 1990.

Navarro, Mireya. "Counting the Homeless: A Lonely, Iffy, Wary Job." *New York Times,* March 22, 1990.

Nelson, Jill. "The Coming of Age of a Homeless Youth." *Washington Post,* October 12, 1989.

"The New Poor: Jobless and Homeless in the United States." *The Futurist,* March/April 1986.

Novak, Michael. "The Homeless at Christmas." *Forbes,* December 25, 1989.

Phillips, Michael. "The Door Is Shut." *Humanist,* May/June 1989.

O'Connor, Colleen, Andrew Murr, and Pat Wingert. "Affluent America's Forgotten Children."

"On the Street of Broken Dreams." *UN Chronicle,* September 1989.

Rabinovitz, Francine F. "What Should Be Done?" *Society,* May/June 1989.

"Rays of Hope For the Homeless." *America,* January 14, 1989.

Relin, D. O. "Lives on Hold." *Scholastic Update,* February 10, 1989.

Roberts, Sam. "Cleanup Drive With a Heart Alters Midtown." *New York Times,* November 30, 1989.

Roha, Ronaleen R. "Giving Back." *Changing Times,* March 1989.

———. "What It's Like To Help the Homeless," *Changing Times,* July 1989.

Rowan, Roy. "Homeless Bound." *People,* March 5, 1990.

Schmitt, Eric. "Plan Upgrades Schooling for Homeless." *New York Times,* May 8, 1989.

Schutt, Russell K. "Objectivity Versus Outrage." *Society,* May/June 1989.

"Science & Society." *Science News,* November 4, 1989.

Settle, Mel. "Must We Tear Them Down?" *Humanist,* May/June 1989.

Sharpe, Leslie T. "Hushing the Homeless." *Psychology Today,* December 1989.

Shuger, Scott. "Who Are the Homeless?" *The Washington Monthly,* March 1990.

"So They May Have a Happy Childhood . . ." *UN Chronicle,* September 1989.

"Social Science and the Citizen." *Society,* May/June 1989.

Spring, Beth. "Home, Street Home." *Christianity Today,* April 21, 1989.

Sullivan, Cheryl. "Foster Care Doesn't Guarantee Safety." *Christian Science Monitor,* September 27, 1988.

———. "Troubled Children." *Christian Science Monitor,* September 26, 1988.

Talese, Gay. "The Homeless Woman with Two Homes." *New York Magazine,* October 30, 1989.

"The Unhealthy Homeless." *The Futurist,* July/August 1989.

"The Unwanted Children of Times Past." *U.S. News & World Report,* May 1, 1989.

Toelle, Miriam E. "The Salvation Army Playschool and Home Visiting Program." *Children Today,* September/October 1988.

Trillin, Calvin. "Uncivil Liberties." *The Nation,* February 13, 1989.

Trippett, Frank. "Down and Out in L.A."

Tumposky, Ellen. "Horror-Hotel Scandal." *New York Post,* November 7, 1989.

Turbak, Gary. "Born, Raised . . . Thrown Away." *Kiwanis,* November/December 1988.

Unsworth, Tim. "Shelter Diary: Help Me Make It Through the Night." *U.S. Catholic,* February 1990.

Van Scott, Miriam. "No Place to Call Home." *Good Housekeeping,* January 1990.

van Vliet, Willem. "The Limits of Social Research." *Society,* September/October 1989.

Vuyst, Alex. "Self-help for the Homeless." *Humanist,* May/June 1989.

Weiner, Melissa Balmain. "Homeless Children Struggle With Their Own Class Struggle." *Orange County Register,* July 2, 1989.

Wells, Stuart. "Preschool Program in New York Reported to Surpass Head Start." *New York Times,* May 16, 1990.

Whitaker, Leslie. "Helping Them Help Themselves." *Time,* February 26, 1990.

Whitman, David. "Shattering Myths About the Homeless." *U.S. News & World Report,* March 20, 1989.

Whitman, David, Jeannye Thornton, Joseph P. Shapiro, Gordon Witkin, and Steve L. Hawkins. "America's Hidden Poor." *U.S. News & World Report,* January 11, 1988.

Wright, James D. "Address Unknown: Homelessness in Contemporary America." *Society,* September/October 1989.
———. "Science, Passion and Polemics." *Society,* May/June 1989.

MISCELLANEOUS

Interview with Martha MacDonald, Norwalk, Connecticut, City Welfare Department, May 26, 1990.
Jennings, Peter, ABC's "World News Tonight," May 17, 1990.

INDEX

ABOUT THE AUTHOR

Joan J. Johnson is a high school teacher in Connecticut. She is the author of *America's War on Drugs, The Cult Movement,* and *Justice,* published by Franklin Watts.